The
Halcyon
Island

The Halcyon Island

Anne Knowles

HARPER & ROW, PUBLISHERS

NEW YORK

Cambridge
Hagerstown
Philadelphia
San Francisco

1817

London
Mexico City
São Paulo
Sydney

Library of Congress Cataloging in Publication Data
Knowles, Anne.
    The halcyon island.

    SUMMARY: While on summer vacation, a boy overcomes
his fear of the river with the help of a mysterious
friend.
    [1. Fear—Fiction.   2. Friendship—Fiction]
I. Title.
PZ7.K7618Hal 1981   [Fic]   80-7909
ISBN 0-06-023203-X
ISBN 0-06-023204-8 (lib. bdg.)

The
Halcyon
Island

One

As Ken came in from the garden he heard them arguing. No, that wasn't true. He heard his father arguing and his mother being in receipt of it: his father's voice brusque and irritable, which meant that he, Ken, was more than likely the subject of the conversation. This had been so ever since they had arrived at Lawnside for their vacation, and that seemed like a good many weeks, rather than the handful of days it really was.

Father had gone to a good deal of trouble finding Lawnside and renting it for the summer. He had taken so little time off from his work recently that

3

he had a good long while due to him, and had been determined to spend it by the river: boating, swimming, doing a little indolent fishing, while Mother painted, and Ken . . . ? He was the problem, he was the fly in the ointment; his idiocy, his stupidity, was upsetting Father's plans again.

Ken crept to the dining room door—the voices were coming from there—and listened. There was no point asking for an ear blasting by making his presence known, but he wanted to find out what in particular was the matter.

After only a moment or so's listening, Ken realized that it was Aunt Tilly who was the cause of the argument. There had been a letter that morning to say that Mother's aunt Tilly had died, and Father had been out of temper ever since, because Mother had been asked to go and sort out all the affairs and effects of the old, narrow, brass-and-mahogany house in London, which had been Aunt Tilly's home. Ken had only the faintest childhood memories of it: mainly of heavy, dusty curtains and huge furniture.

Father had been annoyed enough when Mother first read the letter to him at breakfast. He had obviously been fermenting away about it ever since.

"She couldn't have chosen a worse time," he was saying. It seemed to Ken that even Aunt Tilly could scarcely have had much choice in the matter. When Father was being unreasonable, he really did make a thorough job of it. "I shall have to give up all this and help you straighten everything out, I suppose."

There was a murmuring from Ken's mother, but he could not interpret it. Probably she would be telling Father that she was sure she could manage, but Ken knew he'd never hear of it. Mother had run the household all these years, quietly, lovingly, and had at the same time gone on with her painting, which had enjoyed the same sort of quiet success; but still Father thought of her as a not quite practical person, not able to manage without his presence and help.

There was further rising and falling of voices from within, and Ken was just beginning to think that perhaps just for once he was not the prime cause of trouble, when he heard his mother say, "I shall worry about the river, Peter, if we both go off and leave Ken. Perhaps he should come too. Mrs. Morris says she'll look after him, but she can't be expected to . . ." There was an eruption of noise in the room, which combined an impatient exhalation of breath and the crashing of a fist on some hollow surface.

"I've paid for this house for the summer. I'm

not wasting my money. We won't be away long, and Ken can stay here. I don't want him cooped up in your aunt's old mausoleum. He needs air and exercise."

"But the river . . ."

"The river!" Father was shouting now. "The boy won't go near the river without me here. If he goes off anywhere it'll be as far from the river as possible. He stands as much chance of drowning as . . . as . . . a camel in the desert."

The old theme again. Ken had dreaded coming to Lawnside: knew his father dreamed of them boating together, of Ken's overcoming at last his terror of the water. You might as well ask a claustrophobe to spend a holiday in a stuck elevator. The voice was thundering on.

". . . thought I'd get rid of this nonsense once and for all: You know that was at the back of my mind coming here . . . never get over it if he doesn't face it sometime . . . wasting my time . . . might have known . . . wasting my time . . . and now this happens . . . really too much." The sound came and went and Ken knew his father was pacing the floor. He imagined that Mother would be sitting on the window seat, her hands in her lap, watching him pace and turn, pace and turn. Ken heard her voice, defensive, placatory, and then his father's snort of impatience. He turned away, miserable. He had heard no good of himself. Served him right for eavesdropping.

Father was right, of course. Ken was frightened sick of the river. Even the smell of it in the green willowy garden made his throat tighten with fear, and he could feel the drowning sensation at the back of his nose. So if they were going away he could be free of it for a while: perhaps build up a fund of courage to see him through the long summer at Lawnside. He brightened at the prospect of doing what he liked, though it seemed a kind of disloyalty to wish his parents away. Even Father. He was O.K., really. Ken was used to his irritability in general. It was just as much part of him as his habit of tidiness—not inherited by Ken—and his wholehearted pursuit of any hobby he took up. When one of these coincided with an interest of Ken's, like his model airplane phase, then everything was fine, and there was a closeness between them which was not describable, but very satisfying. But this business of the river, of learning to swim, had been between them so long. Father could swim like a fish; had medals for it. He had been taught when he could scarcely walk and had never known what it was to feel unsafe in water. He had not been with Mother and Ken the day the *Viking* went down.

It had been a seaside holiday, somewhere on the Welsh coast. Ken had shadowy memories of sand and donkeys, and Punch and Judy. He was three years old. Father had gone fishing for mackerel off the end of the pier and Mother had decided, on the spur of the moment, to take Ken on a trip around the bay.

They had crowded too many people aboard. Afterward the boat-rental company was fined and went out of business, but that was not much comfort to the passengers who spent a cold and terrifying half hour in the water, supporting themselves on anything they could find. Ken was not sure how much he actually remembered, and how much was his mother's retelling of the incident to Father, to horrified friends and relatives, to reporters from the local press. He remembered what it was like to be drowning, though, and the terrible feeling of water in his lungs, before he became unconscious, and so unaware of his mother dragging him to a floating duckboard, holding him onto it with all her strength, waiting for the inshore lifeboat. He had been taken to the hospital and put on a respirator. For a while his mother could not believe he was not dead, she often told him later. Perhaps she spoke of it too much. After a while Father would not allow the matter to be discussed at all. "It's all in the past," he would say, and so the doors were shut and mostly it was forgotten, until something set the old fear knocking and hammering again. It happened whenever he got into swimmable water. He felt the sensation of drowning as one senses an enemy without seeing him, and he did not want to come across that enemy again. To avoid it, over the years he had put up with the expected and acceptable taunts and ragging of his friends, the well-meaning persuasion of teachers, and his father's exasperation. This holiday was to have been dedicated to Ken's conversion into a water baby by his father: a bit of an elderly baby at twelve years old, Ken thought. Father had come to Lawnside with the zeal of an evangelist.

Ken was glad he would have a few days' peace before the inevitable. He pictured himself, safe in his father's absence, turning his back on the broad green ribbon of water that lapped the stone edge at the end of the lawn, and exploring the rough wilderness behind the house, unimportant and neglected because it was not "river frontage." There was a fruit and vegetable garden too, and various sheds and outhouses that might be worth looking into. He would saunter about in the village and look for some company his own age. He could go off on his bike down the lanes. At least Father had let him bring his bike. He began to feel comfortable inside at the prospect of having no one to please but himself. He did not think Mrs. Morris would expect much of him except to keep his room straight and to appear for meals, and the latter was no hardship: She was the best cook Ken had ever come across. She lived in a self-contained apartment that was part of the house, and she came as part of the bargain when you rented the house. Mother hadn't been too happy about that to start with. She wasn't used to "help," but Mrs. M. was neither cleaning woman nor housekeeper in attitude, and it had started to work really well. What's more, Ken's father was just the smallest bit in awe of Mrs. Morris, though Ken was not sure why, except that she treated his irritability as if it were some kind of tantrum, and would wait, like a patient nanny, for him to come to himself again whenever he was particularly irascible.

Ken liked Mrs. Morris a lot, and hoped there would be times when he could sit and chat with her, over her ironing board or the mixing bowl, and listen to her stories about her own children, all grown and gone now.

"And what I say, and I'm not the first one to

say it, I know," she had confided in him on their first conversation on the subject, "is you should have 'em, love 'em, and leave 'em be." He knew she would leave him be, too, if he wanted it. There were sensible people in the world, but they were a rare find.

Ken's pretended surprise at his parents' announcement that they were going away for a few days was masterly. It pleased him, this small piece of playacting. It was so much easier than genuine surprise, which was so often tinged with something uncomfortable. He expressed just the right amount of regret at their going, without overdoing it, lest his mother change her mind about it. He could see that she was still worried, but she did not mention her fear about the river, and if Ken did, to reassure her, it would sound suspicious. He gave her hand a squeeze and grinned at her when it was time for them to set off, though, as if discreetly inviting her into a conspiracy, and there was a fleeting expression in her eyes that seemed to show she understood something of what he felt. It was a shame Father didn't realize just how bright she was.

The house was very quiet after they had gone. Mrs. Morris was shopping in the village. Ken walked about the house looking in all the rooms. He had seen it all before, of course, but it seemed subtly different now that he was alone in it, just as one's own familiar house looks different after a long time away. It was a big house, and he felt he wanted to establish a base for himself in it: an entrenchment against the possibility of feeling lonely, though he thought he probably wouldn't feel lonely, as he was used to his own company. It was a rambling, ill-planned house, in no particular architectural style, but solid, as befitted a "residence," which in the advertisement it had declared itself to be. "Spacious riverside residence." It had little character: not the sort of place any respectable ghost would see fit to haunt. Its sole function was to house river lovers comfortably close to the beloved. So wedded was it to the water that nearly all its many windows were turned to look at it, and there was a balcony from which a wider view of the river might be seen, and under that a veranda, for the same purpose, and for resting after exertions in or on the water.

There was no garage for the users of the house, though there was a place at the back near the garbage cans and the kitchen door where a car could be parked. There was a large boathouse, though, with architectural features similar to those of the house—pseudo "timbering" of a generous kind, and a gable end faintly reminiscent of a cuckoo clock. In the boathouse, a blunt black punt and a wooden canoe were tied up. You had to say "tied up," Ken supposed, thinking about it. They couldn't be said to be "anchored" because they hadn't got anchors, and "parked" was too vehicular a word. "Moored": Was that it? He dismissed the boats from his thoughts, and the aptness or otherwise of the word his mind had been searching for, and turned away from the front rooms of the house, their ceilings stippled with river light. He knew which room he wanted. It was small and snug at the back of the house and overlooked the vegetable garden and a distant prospect of woods. He would move all his things in there, out of the balcony room where his father had put him. He did not think Mrs. M. would mind. After all, there'd be less to clean in a small room, and he'd think of something for when Father got back. Perhaps he could say a swarm of bees settled in his old room. That sounded unlikely, but something would suggest itself, he was sure.

He lugged all his clothes and possessions across, and brought over the sheets and bedding. Then he opened the window and looked out. The kitchen window was immediately below. There was a good smell of cake coming from it. Mrs. Morris was obviously back from the shops and preparing the sort of consolation for his parents' absence that she thought Ken would most appreciate. Good old Mrs. M.

For a day or so the village and the surrounding woods occupied his time. It was a handsome village, its timbers as authentic as Lawnside's were phony, and it still had a few proper shops as well as the inevitable antique shops full of dark furniture and warming pans, and Gifte Shoppes crowded with tatty useless stuff that somebody must buy, though Ken couldn't think why they'd want to. There were reproductions of hectic-colored paintings among the varnished brass and plastic ornaments. Ken remembered the face his mother had pulled when she saw them. She was no mean painter, his mother. The things she did best were muted, washed landscapes, delicate, but with no weakness. There were bones in her paintings; structured, fine, not just something of nothing.

It was not a good hunting ground for friendship in the village, though. Perhaps most families were away somewhere else on vacation. He saw one or two little kids playing with a ball, and a group of giggling, toffee-nosed girls who stared at him as he cruised past on his bike. He heard the sound

14

of rock music pulsing out from an open garage, but the lad who was bending over the motorcycle inside was half again as old as Ken and glowered at him from an oil-streaked face and told the air above Ken's head something unrepeatable about the carburetor.

So Ken rode for lonely miles on his bike, in gray cool weather that matched his mood. He enjoyed the feel of the wheels on the asphalt, the effort of uphill pedaling, which was never too strenuous on these valley roads. He played kids' games to himself that he would never have dared in company. He played seeing how far he could count to before he saw a brown-and-white cow; he played getting to a distant tree before he had been overtaken by a car—they were country lanes with little traffic, so mostly he won this game. He pretended his cycle was a motorbike and imagined his hand on the throttle, letting the monster accelerate, feeling the power of it. He was happy, in a low-key, thoughtful way. He didn't feel any need to get very excited about anything, but he was by no means bored. He met few people, except in cars, and they were virtually invisible behind the tilt of the windshield that reflected only clouds or overhead leaves. The few figures he saw in nearby fields or on the road he raised a hand to in salute, and for the most part got a greeting in return.

In the evenings after supper he sat in Mrs. Morris's apartment and chatted with her. She knitted enormous hairy garments for her husband in the Merchant Navy, and while she knitted, she listened to what Ken had been occupying himself with, and told him stories of her own life, and if they grew tired of talking she would turn on the radio. She liked the funny programs best, and her laughing filled the room and made Ken laugh too. There was television in the big sitting room in the main house, but somehow they didn't bother with it. Mrs. Morris wouldn't have it in the apartment.

"Never liked the thought of that great eye looking at me," she told Ken.

"Like a Cyclops," he said.

"Cyclops?" she repeated. "That was our Tim's first boat, the *Cyclops*. He named it after some story he heard at school. Him and his Dad made it. Little canoe she was, and ever so nippy. Tim took her all the way upriver one summer, when he'd be about your age I suppose."

"Your eldest, isn't he?" Ken asked.

"Yes. Master at Arms in a frigate he is now, and big enough to push over a bus. He's the only one took to the sea like his Dad. The others are landlubbers like me, though I enjoy a row in a boat now and again."

Ken looked as though he might be going to say something, but didn't. He sat and listened to the companionable clicking of needles, and thought about where he would cycle to the next day.

In the morning, though, when he was in one of the village shops, buying groceries for Mrs. Morris and paperbacks for himself to read in bed—for Lawnside's library ran only to matched sets of the less interesting classics, with ornate bindings, and minute print in a horrible typeface—it began to rain, and by the time he got back to the house, cold rods of it were beating him through his shirt, enough to take his breath away. Mrs. Morris bustled him into the kitchen, and he was glad of the warmth from the stove. She gave him a cup of hot tea and went into the main house to get him some dry things. It was pleasant in the kitchen: like being in a warm cave. Outside the day was almost sinister, the sky was so dark with clouds. The rain poured down, steadily, insistently, taking the color from everything.

"That takes care of your outing," Mrs. Morris said cheerfully, as she came in with his dry things. She threw the clean shirt and jeans to him, and hung up the wet things he stripped off on the rack over the stove.

"Only the ducks'll be out in this," she said. "You'd be welcome to stay in here with me while I do some baking if you won't think that's too dull."

"I'd like to," he said.

"Right-o then. It won't last more than today, the man on the weather said. It's going to change and get warmer. Not before time. I'll be glad to see the back of these clouds and cold winds. I like summer to warm my bones a bit. I like a good excuse to sit in a deck chair and watch the river."

"It was a good summer last year," Ken said.

"Yes, wasn't it? We had people staying here then that didn't like me sitting in the garden. Perhaps they thought I made it look untidy. Asked me very nicely not to."

"What cheek," Ken said.

"They paid for the house," she explained. "They paid for me. So I suppose they paid for me not to sit in the garden. I missed it though."

"It seems rotten to me."

She laughed. "Not worth worrying about. Your ma and pa won't mind if I sit in the garden. That's probably why the weather's gone so cold!"

She went to the larder to fetch flour and salt

and yeast to start the bread, and Ken called out
to her.

"Mrs. Morris?"

"Yes, dear?"

"You really like the river, don't you?"

"Yes. That's one reason I took this job."

There was a pause. She put flour and salt in a
bowl, and put yeast and sugar in some warm water
to work. Ken watched her hands, moving deftly,
to the purpose. He took a deep breath.

"Have you ever known anyone who was afraid
of it?"

Mrs. Morris walked across the kitchen, her back
to Ken. She realized her answer was important to
him. She had liked the boy the moment she set
eyes on him, which was more than she could say
for some she'd had at Lawnside. She knew a fair
bit about boys, and it had not taken her long to
see where the trouble lay between Ken and his
dad.

"The river? Afraid of the water, do you mean?"
She reached up to a shelf for loaf pans, and set
them on the table. She clattered about a little, considering the matter.

"Bound to be plenty of people feel like that. I
don't much like putting my head under, myself.

Half a second under and I feel I'll explode, and it gets up my nose and makes my sinuses go funny. My boys say I swim like a rubber duck. You should see me!"

"I don't like the water," Ken said quietly, almost hoping not to be heard. Mrs. Morris knew that perfectly well.

"Don't you?" she said. She had heard Ken's father shouting at him. Privately she thought it was mad, pushing the boy to do something he didn't want to. Peter Holmes was a bit of a bully, in her opinion. Anyone could see with half an eye that Ken was not just wary of the water, but really terrified. She went on with her work, hoping he would say more, but when he remained silent, she said, "You stick to the things you enjoy doing, then. You never seem at a loss for amusement, and there's plenty to see around here: some marvelous old churches and houses, if you like that sort of thing, and there'll be a fair in Calverton in a few weeks. Always is, last Tuesday in August. Now, I'll set this bread dough to rise and you can give me a hand with the biscuits."

The whole of that day was like a siege, with wind and rain beating against the windows. Ken enjoyed himself immensely, watching Mrs. Morris at her cooking rituals: "helping" her, as he used to help his mother when he was a little kid, tasting mixtures, scraping bowls, eating crumbs and broken bits from the edges of biscuits. He could not bring himself to talk more about the river, though.

Next morning, when he went to the window, he found the big battalions had retreated, leaving soaked grass and brimming puddles, and dead twigs scattered everywhere. The air had a warm smell to it, and the sky was clear above, with mist curling at the edges where yesterday's wet was already being drawn up by the sun. He got dressed and went out into the garden, and knew for certain that it was real summer now: proper vacation weather. He hoped it would last.

Two

It did last. Each day seemed warmer than the one before, so that cycling, except in the early morning, seemed too much of an effort. Ken idled in the vegetable garden, picked raspberries and ate them until their luscious flavor began to pall. When his parents phoned and said that they would be away longer than they had first intended, he felt oddly disappointed, and that made him realize that he was becoming discontented with his own company, and he could hardly plague Mrs. Morris all the time, now there was so little excuse to hang about in her kitchen. He thought of his school friends:

Thomas Aycott, off somewhere exotic with his father; Peter Wately, in the trailer at Bude with all those hordes of brothers and sisters; Jim Peel doing something energetic—rock climbing, probably. He wished his own father were a bit more adventurous. Mind you, he was a lot older than some people's fathers and he was O.K. when it came to handling boats and swimming: the very things Ken wished to be as far away from as possible. What a stupid, unfair sort of world it was.

Ken tried to imagine which of the three boys he had just been thinking of he would prefer to see coming up the path at this moment, to share this unwanted place with him. He wasn't sure. Friends changed in different surroundings, he knew that. Just as someone could be a friend when it was just two together, and seem suddenly hostile among a crowd. You had to be wary. Ken wasn't one for clubs and rules and ceremonies: They made him uneasy, and sometimes even afraid, in spite of himself, though he would never show it, and was as prepared as anyone to put up a fight for himself—either in words, or in all-out battle which had nothing to do with the boxing his father had taught him, but was more like a cross between Apache warfare and a crude form of jujitsu. He was small for his age, but no one took him on lightly.

He was drifting about in his own idle thoughts when he heard the sound of laughter, coming from some distance, but clear and inviting. He walked around to the front of the house, and realized that the voices were being carried from some way up-river, and he could hear the sound of splashing. He stood at a distance, and watched, though the smell of the water made him uneasy. There was always a smell to water: the harshness of the chlorine at the pool, the huge saltiness of the sea, and this river smell of mud and weeds and overrich green-ness. He shivered a little, but continued to look, as an animal might; feigning nonchalance, but ready to run off.

There was a great deal more to see than there had been when they first came to the river: The cool, unseasonal weather had not been inviting, but this was the first Saturday of the good weather, and various small craft came past as he watched. There was music, too, from transistors in boats that drifted by, and in a punt a young man was playing a guitar to his girl friend. Like the Owl and the Pussycat, Ken thought. A small motor cruiser came by then, its sudden wake setting the punt bobbing and flus-tering a small family of ducks that had upended themselves nearby. The people on the cruiser called out to Ken, and waved. He stared at them. Their sunny, holiday mood made him feel churlish. He wished . . . He did not know what he wished. He half raised his hand, decided not to bother, and mooned back into the house.

Next morning, though, he felt drawn to look at the river again. He was very much surprised at himself, but it seemed all right, with no one there to propel him toward it if he wanted to turn back. It was rather like going to the dentist when you hadn't made an appointment. If you changed your mind it wouldn't matter and no one would be any the wiser. What an idiot they'd think him at school. Still, he suspected sometimes that more people were more scared of things than they'd ever let on. Like Tom Aycott, for instance. Ken was about the only one who knew how he had to go to the john and be sick every time it was a P.E. lesson where they'd have to climb the ropes. Ken had found him there once, all green and shaking. He's got more guts than me though, Ken thought. At least he went and climbed the damned ropes afterward.

The river sparkled in the early light, dispelling the sullen greenness that had made it seem so gloomy and forbidding before. It seemed as if stars shot fire from it, and from a distance even Ken had to admit the beauty of it. He went a little nearer, cautious as a cat.

Then he saw movement under the trailing willow branches that hung down over the far bank, and a boat came shooting past: a canoe, a wooden one like the one in the boathouse. Yesterday, he had seen several of the more usual kayak canoes, fiberglass and canvas, in electric colors, light and handy, in which people rode the river as if on horseback, using their bodies for balance and control. He had realized the skill of it, almost with envy, but knowing he could never achieve it.

The boy in this canoe could handle his craft too, using the paddle as steerage and oar; its short flat blade tucked close astern of him as he thrust the boat through the water, trailing silver drops from the blade edge at the completion of each stroke. He saw Ken standing in the Lawnside garden, and unable to spare a hand for a greeting he called out "Hallo!" and grinned as he went by, leaving the river empty except for the duck family grobbling for worms in the mud of the bank. It was very, very quiet after that, and Ken could feel the sun gathering its strength, drying up the dew. It was going to be a scorching day.

He went around to the back door, and could hear the churning of the washing machine, and the voice of Mrs. Morris singing a nautical-sounding ditty.

"Just had a letter from my big lad," she said to him. "Steaming across the Mediterranean he says he is, lucky feller. Still, I don't see it'll be much hotter there than it's going to be here today. You throw me down anything wants washing, will you, dear? I want to get it done early today. Breakfast won't be a sec."

By midday, the sky was as deep a blue as any Tim Morris's ship might be sailing under, Ken thought. Though she didn't *sail*, did she, with never a shred of canvas on her. Funny how they stuck to the old word. In the Lawnside garden the air felt drowsy, and bees came blundering among the heavy heads of the flowers in the herbaceous border. Ken felt too lazy to do anything at all but lie on a blanket on the lawn with his lunch and his paperback. It was very pleasant, very self-indulgent, like reading in the bath. His father would have been annoyed to see him. Ken grinned. Though it was nothing Father could actually grumble at, like catching him watching TV when he was supposed to be doing homework.

When he had filled himself up with ham and salad

and apple pie with a piece of cheese on, and when he had read until the sun on the white page made the print dance, he rolled over onto his back and stretched himself, gazing up into the sky until he seemed to swim in the incredible, clean, uncluttered blue of it. If only the water were like this, inviting, and not threatening, then he might not be afraid. But he was afraid, because he knew the moment the water took him off his feet he would know once again what it was like to be drowning, even after all these years. He was most dreadfully certain of that.

"My father," Ken announced to himself, "thinks I'm pathetic. Perhaps I am," he said, aloud and defiant, to the terror of a pair of moorhens who had come jerkily up from the bank on their little thin legs, knowing a picnic when they saw one.

"Did you say something, dear?" A large washing-basket was approaching at a slow and rolling pace, hiding its bearer, Mrs. Morris, almost entirely from view. Mrs. Morris's legs appeared to be the legs on which the basket proceeded, which in a way they were. Ken thought he'd better go and help.

"I've run out of lines at the back," Mrs. Morris announced. "You won't mind if I rig some up here, will you? Between these willows the sheets'll get a bit of sun."

"I'll help you," Ken said.

"Tie the line with a clove hitch," Mrs. Morris instructed. Ken looked at her blankly.

"Landlubber!" She laughed. "I'll show you."

She showed him how to turn the line around the tree.

"Did Tim teach you that?" Ken asked.

"No." She laughed again. "Learned it in the Girl Guides. Don't expect they use it much for washing lines in the Navy!"

The sounds of idle, waterborne conversation came from the river as a gaggle of punts went by, full of young men and girls, and one very wet dog which plunged time and again into the water to retrieve a ball, and was then encouraged by each punt in turn to climb back into another, to soak the occupants with the shaking of his shaggy coat. Mrs. Morris was now spreading out pillowcases on the lavender hedge.

"Up to their larks, that lot," she said. "They'll end up wetter than they meant. My, but they do look cool though. I think I'll go and put my feet in the water a bit after all that standing about waiting for that washing machine to finish." It was a very posh automatic machine that the owner of Lawnside had had installed, but Mrs. M. was sure it took longer if she didn't keep an eye on it.

Now, when she'd emptied her basket, she went and sat down on the stone edge, took off her shoes and stockings, and dangled her legs down in the water.

"That's a treat for my bunions," she called back to Ken. She looked very funny, with an expression of mingled pleasure and relief on her face.

The next day seemed as though it must be the crest of the heat wave. The air out of the shade was too hot, and Ken was driven to sit under the shadow of the willows that overhung lawn and water. He found that, despite himself, he enjoyed the quiet lapping of it, and it made one feel cooler, just to look into the shallows.

The canoe he had seen previously drifted by, going slowly with the current. The boy was lying full length in it, on cushions, or a mattress of some kind—Ken couldn't quite see. He looked very comfortable. The paddle was shipped and idle, and he was reading a book. One hand played on the surface of the water, the fingers making shallow, transitory furrows on the smoothness of it.

Ken felt oddly irritated that the boy should be so content, so self-contained and obviously at peace in his element. Ken wanted to break the mood,

to shout something offensive—not rude, just nee-
dling, like "Oy! Ophelia!" or "Who's the Lady of
Shallott, then?"

He got as far as taking enough breath in to shout
either, or both, of these yah-boo remarks, but then
he just said "What the hell" quietly to himself and
slumped down, his head on his knees, feeling hotter
than ever. He took off his shirt, but felt no better.
His feet were bare, but the grass was so dry there
was no coolness in it. Perhaps if he put just one
hand in the water . . . ?

It was then that Ken realized he felt challenged
by that boy in the boat, who rode the river, which
was Ken's terror, as if it were some kindly creature.
His skill, his making it look so easy, so enjoyable,
stirred up that restlessness in Ken that he had felt
when the people on the cruiser had waved to him.

"All right, then," he said aloud, and refusing
to listen to the voice of his own panic, he crawled
nearer and lay flat on his stomach as if peering over
a cliff edge. He must look ridiculous, he knew, but
no one could see him. For a moment the weedy
smell of the water stirred a small panic inside him,
but with an effort he stilled it and let his hand sink
slowly to the wrist. The coolness of the water encircled his wrist like a strap, like a tight cuff, and when

he looked down he could see how the small hairs on his skin made marks like insect legs on the surface tension.

"Meniscus," said a small, school-type voice in his head.

"Yesitiscus," he said, and grinned.

His hand seemed to be at an odd angle, as if his wrist were broken, because of the refraction of the light. They'd done that at school too. He was glad he wasn't at school. He was glad, oddly, to be exactly where he was, looking down into the shallows and letting the coolness creep up from his hand to the rest of him. He lay so still the minnows came out from the hiding-places they had dashed to when this large object intruded on them. The water was only about a foot deep and the tiny, glinting fish lay with the sun shining off them, bright against the brown sand. Ken could see the energy quivering through them, ready to whisk them away at the least disturbance. He scattered them with the shadow of his hand on the water, and then counted the seconds until they regrouped.

When he was tired of this game he walked about in the garden awhile. The air seemed a fraction cooler now, for enough breeze had got up just to stir the willow trails a little. He poked about in the outbuildings, but could find nothing new, and there was a note pinned to the back door saying Mrs. Morris had gone to Calverton and would be back by teatime. She hadn't come and told him. Perhaps she hadn't thought to look for him under the willows. He ambled off, and found himself on the path that led to the boathouse. It was a narrow, concrete path with steps here and there, and a yew hedge that was supposed to be clipped but had got out of hand, rather, and jostled you on either side. It was the sort of path that, once you were on it, seemed to urge you forward to its conclusion. It wasn't that you *couldn't* go back, Ken reasoned to himself, but you felt it more logical to go on.

The boathouse was really just a large, ornate shed, set over an inlet of water, with doors at the back where the path ended, and doors at the front opening onto the river. There was a narrow planked platform running down each side, from which you could step into the boats. The back doors were open but the river doors were closed, making the place dim and dank, though the shady path had taken some of the sun dazzle from Ken's eyes. In the gloom he could see the boats huddled under their canvas. He went in, cautiously, though the planking looked secure enough. The smell of the water was horrible, and it looked oily and sulky through the gaps in the boards. He knew it was only shallow though: just a water floor for the boats to sit on.

Ken uncovered the punt by pulling back the heavy, awkward canvas. The punt, revealed, looked like a long flat pencil box with no lid. There were fat cushions on all the seats, and they looked very comfortable and inviting, even though there was a smell of damp, and possibly mice, about them. Very, very slowly he stepped into the punt, telling himself all the while that he could stop any time he liked. He was wary as a hare, and if fear had flickered up in him then he would have been off and away. But the punt, apart from a slight rocking motion, felt so solid and sat so squarely on the water, with scarcely a degree of tilt as he got in, that he did not feel afraid, but sat down gently on the cushions and rested his hands on the wooden sides. The punt continued for a while the slight movement that his getting into it had set off, but it was not unpleasant, and after a while he moved himself gently from side to side, to feel the boat's response. It was as well no one could see him, moving as gingerly as an old aunty on an ice rink, he thought; but he felt no end pleased with himself. He lay back on the cushions and called out, "I did it then!" to the cobwebby rafters over his head.

He lay still for quite some minutes, and then in his looking about him he noticed the key to the river doors on a nail in one of the supporting timbers. The nose of the punt was tight up against the doors where the lock was. With care he could reach the key, and unlock the doors, without having to get out again. Moving slowly, he accomplished both these maneuvers, and the water doors swung easily outward, for their bottoms cleared the surface by several inches. Now that the space to riverward was open, the whole afternoon was framed in the doorway: water and willows and sunshine, and blue sky, and a streak of more brilliant blue as a kingfisher whisked across the water to the opposite bank. There were soft wet noises of ducks.

Ken took up a paddle from the floor of the punt and brandished it as if he were going into battle. He untied the mooring lines.

"Here goes," he said. His heart was thumping and he felt sick. Then he remembered a story Jim Peel's grandfather had told him about how he was a soldier in the Great War, and how he was only fifteen though he'd told them eighteen, and he'd been sitting in a trench next to some high-up officer just before a battle. There was another soldier there, showing off how brave he was, while Jim Peel's grandfather was so scared he'd wet himself. "Well," said Jim Peel's grandfather, when he told them the story, "this bright lad says to our officer, 'I think you're scared, sir,' and the officer puts a hand on my shoulder and says to the cocky one, 'Yes, I am, and so's this young fellow, and if you were as scared as we both are, you'd have run away long ago.' ''

Well, I haven't run away this time, Ken thought to himself, and he edged the punt out of the boat-house and onto the river. The sensation of the boat under him was strange, and whenever some movement of the water, or of his own body, made it rock too strongly, he felt hot stabbings of fear. Gradually, though, he grew more accustomed to it, and the motion became so pleasant, so effortless, that the flexing of his courage was needed less frequently. The vessel was so solid and steady that it became less important that there was nothing between him and the water but inch-thick planks. She began to drift downstream very slowly, on the lazy current, so he had plenty of time to experiment with using the paddle. Soon his knees were wet from the dripping of it as he changed it from side to side.

The punt moved on, past riverside houses, past reclining figures under trees or garden umbrellas, past croquet lawns, and the playing fields of a school, and a boatyard, with all its little craft tethered, bobbing together at the landing stage.

He still felt apprehensive, as a sensitive rider who

tries out a new horse is: not really afraid, but with reactions set for the unexpected to happen. He still dared not look down too much at the water and kept his mind firmly off the possible depth of it, but gazed about him, concentrating on steering the punt, avoiding other craft, keeping well out of the way of swimmers. He did not want them grabbing at the sides.

When he felt he had gone downstream far enough, he considered how he was to turn around. After some trial and error he discovered that to hold the paddle close in to the side of the boat with the blade resisting the water would swing the punt's nose around to that side, and in that way she could be turned about. It took him a long time, and he was clumsy about it, but he had her facing upstream at last, and began to paddle back. It was only slightly harder work, as the river was flowing very gently, but it took a little more skill to make sure she didn't swing around again to follow the natural tendency of things to go with the stream.

He was really enjoying the rhythm of paddling now. If only he had known it would be like this. He began to whistle and, to keep pace with his own melody, paddled a little harder. Then something—weeds, or some obstruction under the water—twisted the paddle away from him suddenly, and within seconds it was a long gap away from him and the gap was rapidly widening. He watched, horrified, as it drifted away.

Once again he felt sick and all his new confidence evaporated. He was a fool to have thought it was all being so easy. He was near to wanting to cry and angry with himself for the feeling. This was what nemesis felt like, then. You knew that fate would catch up with you one day. You tried to avoid it. Then you got tempted into courting trouble, and sometimes you didn't even realize you were, but it caught up with you all the same. It seemed he was fated to drown, and now he'd drift downstream and go over a weir and that would be that. It did not occur to him to shout for help. It was not anything to do with fear of seeming ridiculous. He did not even think about the number of people he might call out to to save him as he drifted past. He just huddled into his panic and shut his eyes and waited.

"I think you've lost something," somebody said. Ken opened his eyes and blinked. The boy in the canoe was alongside the punt, with Ken's paddle in his hand. He was grinning with amusement, and Ken, pulled abruptly from thoughts of death, felt thoroughly disgruntled.

"You look just like Mole, sitting there like that, with your hands in front of your face."

Ken was small, and squarely built, dark-haired, and he had big hands, like his father. The other boy was skinny as a lath, with wheat-colored hair and sun-browned body covered to the extent convention demanded by a very brief pair of patched shorts.

"Thanks," said Ken, ungraciously, and took the paddle.

"You're staying at Lawnside, aren't you?"

"Yes."

"Were you on your way back?"

"Yes."

"I'll come with you then. I live upstream of you."

"All right."

The boy paddled slowly alongside the punt. "Don't want to interfere," he said, "but a spare paddle's a good idea until you really get the hang of boats. Can you swim?"

Oh God, thought Ken, he's going to push me in. There was no reason on earth he should have thought that. It just came into his head uninvited and unwelcome.

"No," he said, curtly.

"Best to wear a life jacket then. There's probably one in your boathouse. Did you look?"

"No," said Ken.

"Well then, old Mole, have a look when you get back, I should, and next time, don't forget . . ."

"Spare paddle and life jacket. O.K."

They coasted along side by side until they neared the boathouse doors. Getting out had been easy enough. Getting back in would pose problems.

"I'll give you a hand if you like," said the boy, and Ken was not sure whether to be pleased or affronted. He had no time to be either, before the boy had knotted the stern line of the punt to his canoe, and with a skillful leap transferred himself to the punt so lightly and so plumb center that the punt scarcely trembled.

"You move down a bit, and I'll take her in," he said. "It's never easy the first time."

"How did you know it's the first time?"

"I'm always up and down the river, and this punt hasn't been out this season, nor the Lawnside canoe either. You're lucky she's still watertight. They don't take much care of her."

The boy brought both boats alongside the stone edge of the Lawnside garden, and scrambling astern, tied his canoe to a mooring ring, so that he could turn the punt and put her away without the other craft to hinder him. Kent was amazed at how deftly he did it, and knew he'd never have managed it himself.

"I'll leave you to shut the doors. Good-bye." The boy waded off into the water, swam the few strokes to where the shallows began again where the canoe was tied, and scrambled in.

Ken stood on the boathouse platform as the canoe went by upstream.

"Thanks," he shouted.

"See you again," said the boy.

Ken had not even asked him his name.

Three

"My name's Giles."

"That's a bit out of the way," said Ken. They were sitting under the Lawnside willows, with the canoe tied up at the same mooring it had briefly employed the day before. Giles had appeared just as Ken was thinking of risking the punt again.

"I was born when my mother and father were staying in Oxford. There's a road there called St. Giles, did you know?"

Ken shook his head.

"Well, they had rooms there, near the Lamb and Flag. There's a great big fair there for two days, every September."

"There's one in Calverton, in August," Ken interrupted. "Mrs. Morris told me."

"Yes, I know, but that's a small affair, really. The St. Giles one takes up the whole road. Merry-go-rounds and Dodg'ems and birds-on-sticks and furry monkeys on elastic and fat ladies and two-headed sheep, and rifle shooting and cotton candy, and a vast amount of noise. When my mother decided I was likely to arrive they couldn't get the ambulance near, and they had to take her all through the crowds on a stretcher. I don't know whether they called me Giles after the saint, the road, or the fun fair!"

"Do you live where you are now, or are you just on vacation?"

"I'm just here for a while. I'll take you up to the island if you like."

"You live on an island?"

"It's only a little one. There are a couple of small islands about a mile upstream. Swan Island, and Eight Island, where the house is."

"Eight Island?"

"Yes, it's really 'Eyot.' It's an old word for 'island,' so really it's 'Island Island.' Father's named them 'The Halcyon Islands,' because of the kingfishers."

"Halcyon?"

"Halcyons are kingfishers. 'The halcyons brood around the foamless isles.' People used to think kingfishers nested on the water, you know."

"What people?"

"People in the old days. Greeks. They thought when the water was calm and still the birds would hatch out their young on the water. Halcyon days."

"They don't really though, do they?" It occurred to Ken that he had no idea where kingfishers nested.

"No." Giles laughed. "They nest in smelly little holes in the riverbank. They stink of fish."

"Seems a shame. The Greek idea goes better with kingfishers, somehow."

"They're beautiful, aren't they?" said Giles. "But they're real, not mythical. Myths don't have to eat. Kingfishers do. Have you watched them catching minnows? They're brilliant."

"No, I haven't."

"We'll watch them from the island. Can you come?"

"I'd better tell Mrs. Morris."

"All right. I'll wait for you here."

Mrs. Morris was not in the apartment, nor in the main house, so Ken left her a note saying he'd gone out and would be back for tea. He did not say where.

"Could we go in the punt?" he asked Giles. He did not like the look of the frail canoe.

"All right. I'll put my boat in her mooring. Did you look for that life jacket?"

"Yes, there's one hanging up."

"Come on then."

They ran down the path to the boathouse, brushing aside the yew twigs, and opened the doors.

"I'll get the key. You try on that life jacket. It looks O.K."

"All right." Ken unhooked the life jacket, and put it on. The straps were stiff in the buckles, but he struggled with it until he had it adjusted to his satisfaction.

Giles had opened the river doors, and came back to look Ken over. He seemed satisfied.

"Right," he said. "We'll paddle her out, and I'll bring the canoe in here. Two paddles?"

"Two paddles." Ken grinned.

They soon had the canoe at the punt's moorings, and started to paddle upstream, working together.

"Easier with two," said Ken. "You don't get so wet."

"You can turn faster too," Giles told him. "When

45

I say go, you back-paddle while I paddle forward."

"Like this, you mean?" asked Ken, lightly sketching the maneuver he'd made yesterday to turn the punt.

"Right. O.K., now. Back-paddle."

The punt swung around with amazing speed for so seemingly clumsy a craft, making long ripples as she turned.

"Now reverse it," said Giles. "You forward, me back." The punt swung around again and resumed her old course. It was very satisfying to have such control of her, such response.

There was, increasingly, a feeling of casting off civilization as they went farther upstream. Lawnside was, in fact, the last of the riverside houses; and now they were moving between fields, the banks tangled with grasses and summer flowers, except where here and there cattle had their drinking places and had made brown bays of hoof-printed mud, which the recent hot sun had baked hard, holding record of each cloven mark until the next wet spell. One whole fieldful of bullocks caught sight of them as they passed, and galloped parallel with them along the bank, bucking and prancing, tails high in the air, bellowing and snorting through their soapy noses.

On the opposite bank a cat sat disdainfully among

the willow roots, close to the water. Ken saw it yawn, hugely, peeling its face away from neat, white, purposeful teeth. Domesticity sat lightly on it. It was a long way from visible habitation, out on its own affairs. It affected not to mind that the fish, on whom its apparent nonchalance was riveted, had so far been able to elude it, but its tail twitched almost imperceptibly with thwarted hunger. Ken could imagine how the cat might be imagining the feel of curved claws hooked into that inviting silvery flesh. Such thoughts made the saliva run. The cat yawned again, and its tongue explored the edges of its mouth. Then the slight rippling wake of the punt disturbed the surface of the water by its fishing ground, and it stalked off in disgust.

"That's Swan Island ahead," Giles announced. "We'll keep to the right, and you'll see our landing stage."

Eight Island, though bigger than Swan Island, was not very large. The boys tied the punt to the landing stage and Giles led Ken along a weedy path. There were trees, willow and ash, and what had once been a garden, with a wooden bungalow in the middle of it. The timbers were old and green, and seemed all of a piece with the riotous under-growth around it. It was a neglected, secret place, scarcely visible from the river under the trailing branches of the trees.

"We've never bothered much about the garden," Giles said. Inside, though, the bungalow was very pleasant. Lighter than one would expect, somehow, but perhaps that was river light reflected off the white walls. There were books everywhere, and some games and toys, high up on a shelf; and on the walls, a great many paintings of birds, mostly kingfishers: at rest, in flight, preening, fishing. They were very, very good indeed. Ken wished his mother could see them. Giles saw him looking.

"They're Father's," he said.

They went no farther into the house than this one room, which was obviously the room where everyone congregated, whenever everyone was here, whoever "everyone" was.

"Father's not here." Giles seemed to have read his thoughts. "He and James and Philip have gone on. I'll join them later. I don't mind being on my own, and I had one or two things to do."

"My parents are away for a bit too," Ken said. "So we're in the same boat."

"Literally, just now." Giles laughed.

"Where's your mother, has she gone ahead too?"

"Mother left us, not long after Philip was born. She went off with someone. Father brought us up on his own."

Ken could not imagine *his* mother going off with someone; leaving him. It had never occurred to him that she might. Father would make a pretty poor job of things if she did. Maybe that was not fair, Ken reflected. People did rise to occasions, he knew; but then, occasions aren't an entire life.

"I'm sorry about that," he said to Giles.

"Don't worry about it. Come and watch the kingfishers."

In the wildness of the garden was a dilapidated blind, from which they could watch the comings and goings of the little jeweled birds: though not so little, Ken realized, as he had imagined from his more distant view of them. They seemed to be about six inches long, with a workmanlike dagger of a beak. They were brilliant blue above and a sort of terra-cotta color below, with flashes of white on throat and neck.

One bird was sitting on a root at the water's edge. Suddenly it darted, dived, and was almost at once back again, with a small fish held by the tail. With quick strong movements of its neck the bird beat the fish against a rock and vanished again.

"Was that a male?" Ken asked.

"Not sure," said Giles. "They're both so alike, and they're both taking food to their babies now. The nest is below the root. When they were courting he used to bring her fish as a come-on present. This is the second brood. They'll have brought up one bunch already."

"Can we see the nest?"

"Only from the other bank. We can take the punt over if you like."

"O.K."

They went back to the landing stage, and took the punt around the island, letting her run up alongside the bank opposite the place where they had seen the kingfisher perched. A small stream flowed into the river at this point, and Giles eased the punt a short way along it, so that the reeds and rushes disguised it a little. He tied the punt so she would not drift and the two boys lay down flat to watch. They could see the small dark hole in the sandy bank, with a trail of white at its entrance.

"Sicked-up fishbones," explained Giles.

"Lovely," said Ken. "You were right about the smell."

" 'A very ancient and fishlike smell,' " Giles quoted.

"Don't remind me of school," Ken groaned.

"Why, for heaven's sake, should Shakespeare have to remind you of school? It's the last thing Shakespeare would have wanted to remind you of."

"Read a lot of Shakespeare then, do you?" Ken teased.

"Yes." Giles was entirely serious, and there seemed no suitable riposte, so Ken kept quiet, and watched for the kingfisher to come out again. This time both parents came out, one after the other. Pop. Pop. Their fishing skill was incredible. Occasionally, when their obviously ravenous young seemed for a while to be satisfied, they would swallow a fish themselves, head foremost, easy as posting a letter. Even the stickles of the stickleback flowed comfortably down.

Gradually Ken grew stiff, and little itches began to plague him. It was getting very hot again. He huffed out a breath of air, and wriggled.

"Let's walk up the stream a bit," Giles suggested. "The punt's well hidden here, and you needn't wear that thing." He pointed at the life jacket. "The water's not deep."

Ken gladly left the life jacket behind, and followed Giles over the stern of the punt, wading up the cold shallow water of the stream. At least, it was cold at first, but soon the skin grew accustomed to it. It was pleasant, sploshing along. This sort of depth held no fears for Ken. A little farther up the stream the banks curved outward so that the water became more like a little pool.

"Father made this for James and Philip," Giles said. "So they could splash around and be safe."

He stood still in the middle of the pool for a moment, quiet, thoughtful, as if calling something to mind. His thin, brown face and gray eyes seemed entirely remote from any of the happenings of the day. Ken stared, puzzled, not quite comfortable. Then Giles sat down suddenly in the water and thrashed about like a baby. Ken sat down too. It still struck cold to the bits of him that weren't yet acclimatized.

"I'm an otter," Giles said, and rolled suddenly onto his front, submerging his mouth and nose and blowing outward, making a stream of dancing bubbles. Then he took his face out of the water and laughed.

"Try it," he said. "The trick is plenty of breath and keep blowing out."

Ken tried it. Hiding his anxiety, he lowered his chin until the water covered his lips, and blew. It was rather satisfying. Daft, but satisfying. He was reluctant to put his nose under too, and for a moment he thought he wouldn't be able to bring himself to do it, but he did. It was a triumph, but he hid it behind a challenge to Giles to see who could keep blowing the longest. Giles won, but only just.

Then, sudden as a kingfisher, Giles put his whole face and head down through the shallow water and emerged with a pebble in his mouth. He looked ridiculous, and he knew it. He offered no challenge, though. Ken took a huge breath, and lowered his whole face onto the water. His heart was beating very fast. He made himself open his eyes to look for a pebble and discovered it was quite painless, looking under the water. He saw a round and shining stone, only an inch or so away: only a second's plunge to get it. He came up gasping, almost choking on the pebble.

Giles looked hard at him. "Good," he said. It was not praise. Just comment.

Then it became a game, bobbing for stones in the shallow water, shaking themselves like dogs, sending arcs of spray shimmering across the sunlight.

Ken laughed and rolled in the water, and every trace of his apprehension vanished, evaporated, like water drops drawn up by the sun.

"Will you teach me to swim, Giles?" he asked, amazed at himself.

"Of course. Tomorrow, though. Let's walk up the stream a bit farther."

"I s'pose I'd better not be out *too* long," Ken said, "but I did leave a note for Mrs. M."

"She won't be back just yet, I shouldn't think," said Giles. "Come on. I want to show you where the stream starts. It's not far."

They set off farther up the stream bed, between banks of willow herb and hogweed and meadow-sweet. Once a vole came paddling out to midstream, blunt, hairy, and bustling, as if on some important errand. On either side the fields basked in the heat: shaved hayfields, tall whispering wheat, ready for the combine. From stream level you could peer between the stalks, all stiff and ridged at the joints like bamboo. Imagine being an inch high in a forest of wheat. Ken hoped to see harvest mice. He had seen pictures of them, amazingly small and light, with miraculous paws and eyes like jet beads. There were none in sight, though, but he did see a grass snake come down the bank and pour itself into the water, swimming powerfully, like an attenuated S, its tongue flickering.

At the next field edge there was barbed wire across the stream to keep cattle from paddling down to freedom. The boys climbed through. The stream bed grew increasingly pebbly, and then for a while was swallowed up in a tunnel of hawthorns, but it would have been cheating to walk the bank behind them.

"Best take your shirt off," said Giles, taking off

his own as he said so, and tying it around his middle by the sleeves. "There's not much harm done if you scratch yourself, but your Mrs. Morris won't think much of a ripped shirt."

The sun had partly dried their wet clothes, but they got soaked again now, crawling along the stream bed under the clutching thorns. It was very cool under the shade of the bushes, and Ken was beginning to shiver as they headed for the sunlight beyond. When they came out it seemed hotter than ever.

Now there was hardly enough water to walk in and the stream was scarcely more than a brook.

"We're nearly at the source," Giles said.

Within minutes they came to the place where the stream began. The water came welling up out of the ground, from a moss-covered mouth among rocks, spilling down into, and overspilling, a worn stone trough beneath, its stone edge rounded and scoured by centuries of the same movement of water.

Without a word to each other, the boys sat down and watched it. They were quite still. It was such a secret thing, this clear spring from the dark underground. Then they cupped their hands and trapped the achingly cold water as it fell, though neither of them was really thirsty. No one could have resisted drinking it though: so clear and clean and new. It seemed important to drink it.

Then Ken flung the last drops of water from his hands, so that they scattered across Giles's bare shoulders, and he yelled at the sudden sting of them.

"I'll get you for that, old Mole," he shouted, and fell on top of Ken and wrestled with him, rolling him over and over on the grass. He was wiry and lithe and Ken could not get the better of him. He lay in an attitude of mock despair, with Giles's foot on his chest.

" 'Caesar hath conquered the lion,' " Giles crowed.

"I thought you said I was a mole," panted Ken and, grabbing Giles's ankle, tripped him sideways and over.

"A Mole! A Mole!" The war cry trailed off into laughter. It was too hot to fight: too hot to do anything. They lay and baked indolently in the sun, listening to the flow of the water and letting the afternoon slip away.

When Ken got back to Lawnside Mrs. Morris had only just returned. In fact had not even had time to find his note.

"I'm so sorry, my dear," she said. "I do hope you weren't worried. Did you find something to eat, midday? I tried the telephone, but I expect you were in the garden and didn't hear it. I only meant to be out awhile, and then I met Molly Johnson from the Meals-on-Wheels and she was at her wit's end poor thing for someone to help. All her usuals are on vacation and the standby woman fell over somebody's doormat and scalded her arm with stew and had to be rushed off to the hospital. I was a bit worried, I can tell you. It's a while since I drove—though I've always kept up my license— and it's a bit much to start again on a van full of lamb stew and trifle. Still, we managed, and all the old dears got fed, even if it was a bit late. But here's you, supposed to be under my care, and no meal ready for you."

"It's all right, really, Mrs. Morris. I managed O.K." Ken was so relieved that his long day out had not got him into trouble that he did not mention he'd eaten nothing since breakfast. Oddly, though, he hadn't felt hungry. It was only now that his appetite prompted him to ask what was for tea.

She gave him a real high tea "to make up for it." Sausages and mushrooms and tomatoes and chips, and a bottle of ginger beer, and fifteen minutes' worth of a lemon meringue pie.

"My goodness," she said later. "You *were* hungry."

"Mrs. Morris," Ken announced, as if he felt it was something she should know. "I went out on the river today. In the punt."

She looked hard at him, wondering if he really had. It seemed so very unlikely, but he was a truthful lad. Given to daydreaming, maybe, but no liar.

"Well, good for you," she said. She hoped he'd put himself in no danger. She'd never dreamed he'd take a boat out.

"There's a boy lives on an island, not far upstream. I met him a couple of days ago. He came out with me. I wore the life jacket. He said I ought to."

"Sounds a sensible chap," said Mrs. Morris. "I'm glad you've found someone to . . ." She hesitated. "Play with" sounded babyish, insulting to a boy like Ken. "Someone for a bit of company. Ask him in when he comes again. You're going to see him again, are you?"

"Yes. Tomorrow. Do you know them, the people on the island? Eight Island, they call it."

Mrs. Morris thought awhile. "No, my dear, I don't think I do, but then I've only been in this apartment two or three years, and the job keeps me pretty busy. Then when winter comes, most of these river houses are shut up."

"But I thought you'd *always* lived by the river."

"All the while my kids were growing up. Then when they'd spread their wings we sold our cottage and Dad and I took a house in Calverton, but I wasn't happy there. When this job was advertised I asked him should I take it, and he said to go ahead. I missed being by the river."

"Yes, I expect you would," said Ken.

She grinned at him. He looked different somehow. As though he'd grown.

"I'll probably be out quite a while tomorrow," he told her. "Could you make me a picnic?"

She was quite sure she could. "But you'll take care, won't you?"

"Don't you worry, Mrs. Morris," he said.

He stretched his legs out, pushing himself away from the table and patting his stomach. He felt comfortably replete and content. He felt that had he been wearing a waistcoat, he would have hooked his thumbs into it.

"Well, old Mole," he admonished himself, "you've let yourself in for it tomorrow." He was oddly unworried.

Four

They were gliding downstream in the punt. The weather was holding out and the air smelled all August, with the sun beating on the dust of the towpath and the heavy leaves of the riverside trees. There was the smell of the ancient varnish of the punt and the plush of its cushions, and more than anything the exhalation of one's own skin: like new bread where it was dry, and of an applelike fragrance where it had plunged in water.

"Keep her going steadily," Giles said. "I'm going to show you something. Watch me."

He slipped over the side of the punt, swam a

few strokes, and then dropped his head and hung in the water. It held him up, with no effort on his part, but his head was submerged. He hung there for almost a minute, raised his head for air, and then hung still again, with only slight movements of his hands and feet. Then he swam back, put one hand lightly on the punt's side to steady himself, and shook the water from his eyes.

"Ever see a dog that couldn't swim?" he asked. "Or a rat or a weasel or an elephant or a kang—well, I'm not hot on kangaroos, but you know what I mean."

"Well," Ken admitted, "I suppose they do all swim."

"Trouble is, you see," said Giles, "we're the wrong shape. The water holds us up fine, like it does all those other animals, but because we walk on two legs, not four, our center of balance has shifted and when we float on the water the bits we need to breathe with are in the wrong place."

"I wouldn't float like that if *I* fell in," Ken said. "I just know I wouldn't."

"Only because you'd thrash about and upset your balance. Can you ride a horse?"

"No," said Ken, beginning to wonder if he was useless at everything.

"You ride a bike, though. I've seen you."

"Well, yes."

"If you waved your arms and legs about, all over the place, you'd fall off, wouldn't you?"

"More than likely." Ken grinned.

"Same thing then. Now I'm going to swim like a frog, breaststroke, you know. I don't go much on the style of it, but it's good to begin with."

He swam around the punt, slowly at first, and then increased his speed.

"Now I'll shift into top gear," he called, and changed to a rapid and effortless crawl that took him through the water swift as an eel. It was not consciously athletic, like Ken's father's swimming. It was as natural as running, it looked as much fun as a good downhill spin on a bike. Only the element was different. Ken wanted to be able to do that.

"Can I try?" he asked. A week ago he would rather have been handed over to the Spanish Inquisition.

"Let's just get you in the water first. You'll have to take that life jacket off. It'll keep you too upright. I'll get back in. You take tight hold of the stern line, and let yourself down into the water. I'll be just above you, ready to grab."

Now it had come to it, Ken felt a little cold again, and the water, even on such a hot day, felt cold too, and looked deep. However, he took a firm grip on the stern line, and lowered himself cautiously down. He lost his grip on the slippery wood, realized too late he'd given himself too much line, and sank under the surface, into the green semidarkness.

"I always knew you would drown," said his fate, nastily in his ear, and he felt immeasurably and ridiculously sad that he would have no chance now to eat the chocolate cake Mrs. Morris had promised him. She had discovered his passion for chocolate cake. The fact that he would not be there to eat it seemed oddly far more important than the fact that he was about to die. One ought to take one's own death as of more serious consequence, he thought, than the missed opportunity of chocolate cake. Thought whirled and spun in his choking brain for an immeasurable, unendurable length of time. Then a thin brown arm heaved him up on the line and a strong hand grabbed his wrist.

"Idiot." Giles grinned. "Still, you didn't let go of the line."

"How long was I under?" Ken gasped.

"About three seconds."

"What if I'd let go?"

"I'd have come after you."

"Oh."

Looking up at Giles's face, framed in pale hair

like the imagined rays of a star, Ken had no doubt that he would. He was not the sort to say "I'll hold you" and treacherously to remove a supporting hand when you least expected it. Giles was an odd sort of boy, very different from anyone Ken had ever known: clever, but not creepy, and with no Judas element. Friends were a fickle lot, Ken had found. Even the best of them would side against you, one way or another, if it suited their ends. Giles would not. Later, it occurred to Ken, as he lay on the water as he had been shown, allowing himself to be towed gently along by the punt, that he had not thought of nicknaming Giles, who, after all, called him Mole, and was in so many ways the counterpart of the Water-Rat, the mentor and friend of that blundering incompetent gentleman. It wouldn't do, though. Giles was just himself. Ken did not want to turn their friendship into a game: a reenactment of a known plot. Life didn't work like that. He didn't mind being Mole, though. It was a comforting sort of name, and seemed to make it easier for him to deal with his shortcomings as a river boy.

They went on down to within sight of the lock, and Giles drew the punt in to the left-hand bank.

"You'd better get back in now, or you'll get too cold. Come on."

He hauled Ken in as if he were a fish, and they both jumped onto the bank and tied the punt to a tree. Then they raced about on the grass to get warm and dry.

Craft of all kinds were moving in and out of the lock. The boys could hear the clank of the sluice wheels and the creaking of the gates as the lock-keeper pushed them open. It was strange to watch the boats coming upriver bobbing into view as the level rose, and those going downstream vanishing downward into the lock basin when the water poured away through the sluices.

"D'you want a closer look?" Ken asked.

"Yes," said Ken.

The lock smelled of green slime, and of wood that had been wet for centuries. The basin was at low level when they arrived, and looked like a well. There was a small launch down there, with a man and a woman and two or three small children on it. The woman had hold of an iron ring set in the well, and was keeping the boat steady.

"Why don't they just tie the boat up?" Ken asked.

"Think about it." Giles laughed.

When he'd thought about it, Ken realized that when the water started to pour in, the level would rise, and the boat would rise with it, and if it was tied up short, the rope would pull the bows under.

"O.K. I see," he said.

"I went to a harbor once, when I was a little kid," Giles told him. "It was in France, and I saw a notice and I asked my father what it meant. He told me it said 'At high tide this notice is underwater.' I thought that was jolly funny, but it wouldn't be if you'd parked your car next to it!"

The expected torrent had not yet started coming in through the sluices, and yet the air was full of the noise of water running fast and tumbling over.

"What's making that sound?" Ken asked.

"Weir," said Giles. "There's a notice, didn't you see, saying 'Danger.' "

"*Is* it dangerous?"

"Yes," said Giles. They sat on the edge of the lock, watching the boat rise slowly as the sluices opened.

"I'm glad we came. It's fun here," Ken said.

"I wouldn't be anywhere else." Giles was looking into the distance, considering something. "You mustn't be altogether unwary of the river, though. Does that sound stupid, when I've been telling you to trust it to hold you? I'll teach you to swim, and when you can, I'll take you out in the canoe and show you how to handle her, but you must always be a bit on your guard. It's like horses again. An element of danger, always, but no reason to be afraid. Just careful."

He was utterly concerned, and serious, as if he positively wished that no harm should befall Ken.

The water had risen to its highest level in the lock now. The launch was dancing a little to the throb of her engine. The lockkeeper shoved at the long beam of the nearside gate to let her through. Suddenly there was a slithering noise, and a splash, and a scream from the woman on the launch.

"Mike's fallen in!" she yelled, but the lockkeeper had his back to them, and her husband and the other two children were up near the keeper's cottage, where they had been looking at the flowers in the neat garden.

"Quick!" said Giles. "Tell her to switch off the engine." And he was gone, into the water, as suddenly as if he had vanished by some trick.

"Cut your engine," shouted Ken. He wasn't in the habit of shouting at adults, and he was very much alarmed at what was happening, but his voice came out full of authority, and the woman stopped running up and down dementedly and did as she was told, leaping down into the cockpit to switch it off.

Giles came to the surface, clutching the child: a little boy about four years old.

"Grab him," he said to Ken, and as Ken pulled

the child out, Giles scrambled out alongside.

There was a great deal of confusion and running about, and the woman was hugging her son and crying, and the lockkeeper was trying to jolly the father by joking that there was a fine for swimming in the lock, and everyone was praising Ken, who most embarrassedly assured them that he'd done nothing except actually pull the child out of the water.

"And you made me switch off the engine," the woman said. "John told me that's what I should do if anyone fell in"—she indicated her husband, who had brought a blanket to wrap Mike in—"but I was so scared I wasn't thinking. He'd have been pulled down into the screw, and God knows what would have happened."

"It was my friend Giles who really saved him," Ken protested, but Giles was nowhere to be seen.

Ken escaped the fuss as soon as he could, and went back along the bank to the punt. Giles was there, eating.

"I saw you'd brought a picnic," he said. "I've just started on mine."

"What did you go off for?" Ken grumbled. "They all thought *I'd* done the gallant rescue bit. I told them it was you, but you'd gone."

"What does it matter?" Giles grinned. "The kid's safe, and I was wet and hungry. I swear lock water's colder than ordinary river water."

"*Would* he have been caught up by the screw?"

"Most likely. You have to be careful. O.K.?"

"O.K." said Ken. "Have a sandwich."

"No, these'll be fine for me. Then," he said in a put-on prim voice, "we shall wait an hour for purposes of digestion before we continue with our instruction in the natatory arts."

"What?" said Ken with his mouth full of cheese and tomato.

"Swimming," said Giles.

There were dragonflies near where the punt was moored. There were a myriad insects, in, on, and around the river: the inevitable pestilential August flies that clustered about the heads of horses and cattle that grazed the water meadows; the water striders that printed delicate footmarks on the surface of the river; the beetles clutching their bubbles of air as they went below; the honey-seeking butterflies and bees—the working sort, and the big fat, furry bumbles that in theory could not fly at all, and in fact sometimes made a poor job of it. Ken found one, grounded, and persuading it to walk up a piece of reed, flung it skyward again, where it vibrated its stubby wings, found sufficient lift at last, and was away. But it was the dragonflies that fascinated him, with their iridescent bodies and gauzy wings, in such contrast to their science-fiction heads, with those enormous gunmetal eyes. Something about the dragonflies looked mechanical, in spite of their beauty. Ken was not altogether sure that he liked them, though they filled him with admiration.

Giles, who had been half asleep, yawned and stretched himself, and got out to cast off the punt.

"We'll go back upstream a bit," he said. "There's a shallow place with a sandy bottom that should do well for you to learn in."

They paddled together, in no particular hurry, watching the other river users. They were certainly a varied lot. There were obvious holiday folk just out for an hour or so, rowing disastrously and getting in everyone's way. There was an earnest young woman in a racing skiff, counting her strokes as she passed, her cheeks puffed out by her efforts.

"She must be mad, in this heat," said Giles. "Now that's more the style." He pointed to a man in a punt not unlike their own, but he was poling it, elegantly, resting between each easy movement, letting the pole trail in the water.

"Can you do that?" Ken asked.

"Yes, but this punt hasn't got a pole. I checked.

Besides, with paddles, we can both do the work!"

A good-sized cabin cruiser was approaching now, sitting heavily in the water. It had been painted white once, but the paintwork was flaking and streaked with green and with rust marks. There seemed to be close to twenty people on board, all dressed in clothing that looked as though it had come out of granny's attic. Despite her heavy load, the boat was moving fast, with throttle wide, and her wake washed out behind her in a six-inch wave that caught the little racing skiff and nearly overturned her. The girl in the skiff looked very angry, and the man at the controls of the cruiser blew four blasts on his hooter, which seemed the signal for a lot of noisy laughter from his passengers.

"Idiot," said Giles. "That means 'I'm out of control, get out of the way.' They've been nothing but trouble, that bunch."

"I haven't seen them before."

"No, you wouldn't have. They've been farther upriver all week. It's a hired boat, but whoever owns it should be ashamed to let her out in that state. Still they've made no attempt to clean her up themselves, and I've seen them dump rubbish on the bank, and empty their Porta-San in the river. They were taking potshots at the ducks with an air pistol the first time I saw them, but the lockkeeper from Streatway saw them as well and said he'd get the police if they didn't stop. Goodness knows where they're off to now."

Ken was glad when the cruiser was out of sight. They'd looked a rough-looking lot: Something about them made him wish them well away.

The boys paddled on past the houses below Lawnside, and on the opposite bank there was a houseboat moored. It was very plain; just a box, really, upturned onto a shallower oblong box like a bigger, squarer version of a punt. There was a rail around the top of the upper box, and an awning, under which a young woman sat reading a book. She looked up and raised a hand in greeting, and Ken waved back.

"I see the traveling circus has come downstream," she called out, smiling.

"What was that?" Ken asked.

"That lot, in the old *Adventurer*. I thought she was due to be scrapped. She'll need to be, after that lot, if they don't sink her first!"

She went back to her reading, and Giles dug Ken in the ribs to encourage him to paddle faster.

"We're nearly there," he said.

They came to a place on the same bank as the houseboat, where there was a row of mooring posts at the end of a lawn. There were a great many notices saying "PRIVATE," "NO MOORING OR LANDING," "TRESPASSERS WILL BE PROSECUTED," and various other threats and prohibitions.

"It's all right," said Giles. "They're away. It's just ideal here for swimming. You won't be out of your depth at all, and there's no mud or weeds."

Ken was rather doubtful about the wisdom of attaching their punt to a notice saying "NO MOORING," but Giles seemed entirely happy.

"Strip off then," he said. "You don't want to swim in your shirt and your life jacket."

When they were standing waist deep in the water, Giles showed Ken how to move his arms and legs. He'd been told before, but only now could he see the reason for the movements, the turn of the hands on the back-thrust to push you through the water, the froglike impulsion from the strong kicking of the legs.

"Don't be tempted to hold your head too high," Giles warned. "Let the water take most of the weight of it. Blow the water away from you if you need to, like our otter game in the stream."

When he had practiced the strokes, fore and aft, to Giles's satisfaction, Ken lay across the other boy's supporting arms and tried both ends at once.

"That's fine," said Giles. "You're a natural." Ken

by no means felt like one, but he was no longer alarmed by any of the business of being in the water.

"Push off from where you are now," Giles said, "and come toward me. Don't try the strokes. Be a torpedo. I'll be here to grab you."

He did it. "I did it!" Ken shouted. He'd pushed through the water a good three yards on the thrust from his legs, and Giles had caught and held his outstretched hands.

"Do it again," ordered Giles, "and do one stroke this time, just with your arms."

The stroke was a little sketchy, but Ken did it.

"Again," said Giles. "Two strokes this time. Legs as well."

It looked several miles from the place Ken stood to where Giles was waiting.

"Here goes," he said. Two strokes of the arms, stronger this time, and some rather uncontrolled legwork, and he reached the hands again.

"You swam," said Giles.

"I did, didn't I?" Ken waded toward the bank, and sat down between "NO LANDING" and "WARNING. GUARD DOGS" and laughed and laughed and laughed until he ached, and his face was wet with tears.

"If my father could see me," he chortled. "If my father could see me he'd . . ." Ken spluttered for the right phrase and couldn't find it. "Oh, I don't know. Think he was seeing things, I expect. Me. Swimming. He'd have a fit."

Giles looked him up and down, with one eyebrow raised.

"You only did two strokes, you know. Come on, let's go and look at the house."

"We can't go in *there*," Ken protested. "It'll be all locked up."

"We won't go inside," said Giles. "We'll just walk around outside and look in through the windows."

They skulked up the lawn like a couple of conspirators on the way to a murder conference: Giles exaggerating his cloak-and-dagger gait to such an extent that Ken was almost overcome once again with a fit of the giggles, except that there was something just a whit frightening about creeping around quite so prohibited a place. It was all quite ordinary though: not unlike Lawnside, except that the architecture was respectable—and genuine—Georgian. Some of the windows were shuttered, but others could be peered through, and gave a view of silent, shrouded, dust-sheeted interiors that had obviously waited a good while for their owners' return.

"They're in the south of France," said Giles. "On the coast somewhere."

Ken wondered if Tim Morris had passed within

hailing distance of them as he "steamed across the Mediterranean." "Poor old house," he said. "It looks sad, all shut up like this. It seems a waste. They should have let it, or something."

"Probably didn't trust anyone to look after it properly."

They explored the gardens, which were stiff and formal, and showed little sign of neglect.

"There's an old man comes in once a week. Mows the lawns and so on. Don't worry, he won't be here today," said Giles.

The wide gravel path that led to the boathouse here was lined by high clipped hedges of box, as square-edged as their name and most unlike the ragged yews at Lawnside. The boathouse itself had, instead of wooden doors, iron grilles on both inner and outer sides that gave the impression of portcullises, though they swung outward rather than up— or at least, they would have swung outward had they not been securely locked. There was a small but very elegant little motorboat inside, and a very handsome rowing boat as well.

"They must be rich," said Ken.

"Rich enough," Giles agreed. "We'd better go now, before someone makes off with the punt."

Ken was looking about him, carefully, all the way back to the riverbank.

"What's the matter?" Giles asked.

"I was just wondering about the guard dogs."

"In kennels," said Giles.

"Yippee!" shouted Ken, and danced a war dance all over the lawn. He got one or two strange looks from people passing by on the river, but no one bellowed at them to get out, or go away. Ken wondered if they thought he lived in this posh place. He didn't think he'd really like to, but it might be fun for a while.

"We'd better get back now," said Giles.

"You're right."

They pushed off the punt and set off to paddle the last half mile to Lawnside.

"Will you come in for a bit?" Ken asked when they arrived at the boathouse. "Mrs. M. said you'd be welcome."

"Thanks," Giles said. "But I'd better get back. I've got things to do. Tomorrow?"

"Tomorrow," said Ken.

Giles transferred himself to his canoe, and paddled away upstream. Ken watched until the sunlight on the water seemed to swallow up the small craft and its occupant, and then he ran across the lawn to the house.

"Mrs. Morris! Mrs. Morris!" he yelled. "Guess what?"

Five

For the next few days, with the weather glorious as before, Ken and Giles were on and around the river from the first early mist trails to late evening, when reflections of upside-down clouds, sunset pink, glided across the water, looking as tangible as cotton candy. It was hard to think they were only illusions, and the clouds of which they were the shadows, scarcely more than shadows themselves, just water vapor, constantly moving, shifting, colored in further illusion by the reflected light of the sun as the river turned away from it into night. What was real, and what was not real, Ken wondered, watching. Everything was real for the moment it was there, he thought. U.F.O's were real to the people who saw them. Feelings were real though no one could see them at all, or prove them, for that matter. So the water clouds were real, even if they did not, in logic, exist at all, and very beautiful they were, however transitory.

For Ken the river was an unknown country, and he followed Giles as one might follow Livingstone across Africa. Giles knew the landscape and the language of it, had named every curve and inlet and tributary stream. Some of it Ken had seen before, on his bicycle rides, but one saw an entirely different aspect of everything from the river. Roads, churches, bridges, fields were subtly different, as if interpreted by a different painter.

It was an exciting, exclusive world. People seen at a distance, waving, or in vehicles, seemed alien. Those on the banks, allies perhaps, but to be regarded with caution. Ken soon began to know a handful of them: the lockkeeper and his tall son Jim who worked on a nearby farm and could be seen at work on the combines where harvest was beginning, the crews of the steamers that came upriver as far as the lock, the ferryman at the crossing on the reaches above Eight Island, and a handful of hopeful fishermen regularly and patiently squatting on the bank, though it was not ideal weather for fishing.

Ken saw one old fellow, though, just at the moment of triumph, when he landed a fish, a good-sized one, a perch, perhaps. Ken wasn't sure. He just had the impression of gleaming scales in the landing net and the look of supreme and concentrated pleasure on the old man's face. Ken felt he had to call out and congratulate him. Giles was lying asleep, flat out, on the punt cushions.

"That looks a good catch!" Ken shouted, and the old man grinned and waved his battered hat in salute.

Now that Ken's skill with the punt was increasing, and he could turn, reverse, zigzag, come alongside a bank, and move away from it with dexterity, Giles would frequently sit opposite him, sprawled in the heat, his long thin limbs browner and his hair bleached even paler by the sun. He often seemed half asleep, and yet nothing escaped his notice. He pointed out every riverside creature that came into view, knew the names of the waterside flowers and the birds that came to drink and bathe and refresh themselves from the August heat.

He still had new things to teach Ken about handling the punt, too, some new trick with the paddle to make the blunt wooden craft more obedient to

Ken's wishes.

"You can try the canoe soon," he told Ken. "It's more fun. But you must get your swimming a bit stronger first."

Each day they swam: two or three short sessions, stopping before Ken grew cold or tired. He was improving. He was pleased. The froglike movements Giles had taught him got him pleasantly through the water, not fast, but learning to trust the element in which he moved. And always Giles was there to encourage him, to persuade him he could do just a stroke or so more than he'd thought he could. Giles in the water was utterly at home, like the otter he had pretended to be on the day they had explored the stream: like the otter they both hoped they might, with luck, see; searched for for hours in the hope of finding; lay in wait for among reeds and rushes on the bank, still as stones, in the hopes of glimpsing. But for all their patience, all their watchfulness, the most they saw was a possible paw print, a muddy, sliding place that might be, or might have been, an otters' water chute, and once, in early light, a trail of silver bubbles moving tantalizingly ahead of them, and vanishing at their approach.

"It's good to know they're there," Ken said. "Even if you can't see them. I'm *sure* they're there."

81

"So am I," Giles agreed, but they still hoped to see one for themselves.

Mrs. Morris had persuaded herself not to be worried by Ken's long hours away from Lawnside. She had watched him take the punt out of the boathouse and saw with relief that he still wore the life jacket, even though he assured her he could swim a good few strokes now.

A lad with plenty of sense, was Ken, and as for that young friend of his, he must be a proper marvel, to have got him over his fear of the water and even started him swimming. She felt she'd like to see this young Giles and tell him what a good job he'd done, but she had only once been up early enough to watch their crack-of-dawn departure, and then against the morning sun her eyes had been too dazzled to see properly.

It was clear enough that Ken was happy, though; twice the boy he was when he came. When he returned in the evenings he was dog-tired, smelling of sunshine, and full of the day's adventures. He had always finished to the last crumb the picnics she sent with him, but could always find room for his supper. He looked brown and well.

She suspected that, as is the way with boys, his account of his doings was probably edited for her benefit. She would bet on it that he and Giles got up to the same sort of mischief her own lads had done. She remembered how they had admitted to her, years afterward when they were, in their opinion, too old and respectable for her to remonstrate about past misdeeds, that they had often shinned up out of the water onto the decks of steamers and hitched free rides down to Falford and back, and would tell dreadful tall stories to the passengers about how drunk the captain was. They had told her about long vigils up willow trees with peashooters, disturbing the romances of young lovers in punts tethered below; about setting adrift in his rowing boat—having first adroitly removed the oars—one of their more detested schoolmasters who had been unfortunate enough to be discovered by them having forty winks after some brisk exercise on the water.

She smiled to herself. Proper pains in the neck they'd probably been, but it was only mischief, no vice in it—not like the sort of thing so many kids seemed to get up to nowadays. She was sure there was no vice in Ken, though, nor Giles either, and she enjoyed hearing what Ken chose to tell her of their exploits when they chatted together after supper about the places he and Giles had explored, the kingfishers, how far Ken could now swim.

He'd asked her not to mention anything of this to his father. "You won't tell him, will you, if he rings or anything?"

"What d'you take me for?" she said, *tut*ting at him. "You'll want to tell him yourself. I know that. I'm not daft, you know."

"Thanks, Mrs. M."

When his parents did ring, the following evening, and Mrs. Morris called out to him to come and talk, Ken realized with something like shame that he didn't really want to speak to them. It was as if they were invading his newfound world, intruding on him. He could scarcely bring himself to take the receiver and put it to his ear. His mother's voice dispelled this feeling to an extent, though. She sounded so anxious, so concerned for him. She hoped he was all right. He assured her that he was.

Mrs. M. was mouthing something at him.

"Hang on a minute, Mother," he said, and looked inquiringly at Mrs. Morris.

"Don't tell her you've been on the water. She'll only worry."

"She'd only tell Father too. Of course I won't."

He spoke to his mother again, assuring her he had plenty to do, wasn't bored, was eating well, and felt fine. She wasn't to worry.

Father's voice cut in, saying that the whole affair

of the aunt's house was becoming ridiculous; that the old dear seemed to have taken leave of her senses before she took leave of life; that her will needed a whole fleet of lawyers to sort out, and that she seemed to have left property she didn't own to people who didn't exist.

"It's too bad, really it is," his voice went on, familiar in its irritability. "Your mother and I have been landed with coping with the mess, which is why we've been such a long time about it. It's annoying, to put it mildly, wasting my holiday like this. Well, we'll hope to be back in a day or so. Meanwhile, you've been keeping yourself occupied, I hope?"

"Yes."

"Done some cycling?"

"Yes, Father."

"And what else?"

"This and that."

There was a pause, as if his father were taking a deep breath.

"Highly explanatory. I suppose you haven't . . . No, of course you wouldn't . . . We'll see you soon, anyway. Good-bye, Ken."

"Good-bye, Father."

"Take care, Ken," said his mother's voice.

"I will, I will," he said, and put down the phone.

He felt as he did when a vacation was coming to an end: wishing he didn't have to start school again, but knowing he'd get used to it.

He stared for a while at the phone, lying dumb in its cradle, then shook himself free of the thoughts the conversation had stirred up in him, and went out into the evening garden. It was quite late, but still very light and warm. There was no point in going to bed yet, for even his north-facing room felt airless. He would sit on the lawn for a while in the cool.

There were plopping noises of fish rising for a belated meal of water-skimming, unwary insects. Roach, perch, carp perhaps, each sank when replete, encircled by ripples. Ken wondered if fish slept, and supposed that they must.

A swan, ghostlike in the muted evening light, came shimmering by, dipping and preening, one black leg hitched up behind on her white plumage. When Ken had first seen this trick he had thought the bird must be damaged, or deformed in some way, but it seemed a habit with swans. Suddenly, startled by something Ken could not see, she became alert, spread her wings wide and began the strong beat that would transfer her from water to air. Her black webs thrashed momentarily along the surface, until the pinions lifted her, and she flew off upstream, the broad flight feathers making an eerie whistling noise as they pushed down on the air, like the sound of a mournful voice. Ken wondered whether the bird was from Swan Island, and if Giles would watch her come in to land, or rather, to water, when she arrived there.

Mrs. Morris arrived with cups of cocoa.

"Mind if I join you?" she asked, and sat down heavily on the grass without waiting for an answer. "Have a good chat, did you, with your ma and pa?" It had been a bit one-sided, it seemed to her, and none too long, considering they hadn't seen him for a couple of weeks.

"Yes, thanks," said Ken. "They'll be back in a day or so."

"That'll be nice." She wondered if he thought so.

"Hot, isn't it, even out here," she went on. "I'll look for our old tent for you if you like, tomorrow sometime. You could put it up on the lawn and sleep out in it if you like; if the weather holds. I can't think why I didn't suggest it before. It's nice, sleeping outdoors."

"Thanks, Mrs. M. You are a dear."

He's a good lad, she thought to herself, with a deal more to him than that father of his has ever taken the trouble to find out. It'll be one in the

eye for some people when they discover the boy
can swim, and handle a boat, and take care of himself
the way he has. And all because of that young friend
of his. Mrs. Morris was determined to ask Giles
in for a meal. With his father and brothers away
he would probably do with feeding up a bit. It
was odd, she had thought when Ken had told her
about it, that the boy should be left on his own
like that. Not that she was one for fussing over
kids, mind you. Anyway, judging by what he'd
taught Ken, and what Ken had reported to her,
he was obviously one of the sensible sort.

"I'll take the cups in if you've finished, dear,"
she said. "You'll be in soon, will you?"

"Yes, I'm coming," said Ken, and walked after
her to the house. Light was fading now. Only the
river showed silver against the gray, and some white
moths fluttered like bonfire ash in the quiet air.

Six

Mrs. Morris was up more than usually early next morning. Ken was vaguely aware of having heard the telephone ringing when it was only just light.

He heard her moving about in the kitchen below, for his window was open as wide as possible. He had heard the milk arrive, and the opening of the back door as she took it in. He heard the opening and closing of various cupboards and drawers. All these sounds he listened to as he lay idly and comfortably abed, until Mrs. Morris appeared with a cup of tea and a bulky cylindrical object, which rattled slightly as she dumped it on the end of the bed.

"Sorry to wake you so early," she said, "but I've got to go out for a while. I've found the tent for you, look. Took some finding, I can tell you. The poles and pegs are inside. You'll have to work out for yourself how to put it up. I've got to go into Calverton. It's my niece, Mary. She's expecting. Silly girl."

"A baby, do you mean?" Ken asked. He thought that's what she meant, but what was so silly about it?

"That's right, dear. Should have had more sense, but what's done's done, I suppose, and she needs someone with her. Look, if you want a picnic there's chicken in the fridge, and the chocolate cake's in the tin. You'll be back the same time as usual?"

"Round about then, if that's all right."

"You take plenty to eat, mind, and there's more ginger beer in the cupboard, or Coke if you'd rather."

"Thanks."

" 'Bye then, love."

" 'Bye, Mrs. M."

Ken got up and ate breakfast, and then pottered about the lawn with pegs and mallet, putting up the tent while he waited for Giles. It didn't look too bad when he'd finished. A bit lopsided, perhaps.

He grew impatient, waiting for Giles to come, and having gathered together a picnic, he set off in the punt toward Eight Island. It was only just after ten o'clock and he saw hardly a human soul on the river. His company was mostly the whirring insects, and a vole or two, and an old gaunt heron, standing solitary over its shadow, hunched and still. Ken wondered if there were otters. He still hoped he might see one. He moored the punt to the landing stage at Eight Island, and made his way down the path, through the weeds and nettles and elder seedlings. The timber house and the overgrown garden seemed of an equal greenness. The whole place had an air of pleasant melancholy. It seemed set apart from everywhere else, more than by the fact it was an island. He called out near the bungalow and no one answered, so he walked quietly down to the blind to see if Giles was there, and he was, watching attentively, completely absorbed.

"It's me," Ken said in a low voice, not wanting to make him jump, or to disturb whatever was taking so much of his attention.

Giles did not look around, but waved his hand to indicate "Come here and see."

The young kingfishers were out of the nest hole, and were perched, three of them, in a wobbly row on a willow root, looking hopefully about them. After a while one of the parent birds swooped in a shallow dive, returned with a small minnow, beat it against a stone, and presented it to the fledglings. The one to move quickest got the fish and started to swallow it. It was a small fish, but big enough for the young bird to find some difficulty with. It paused momentarily with the meal halfway down, reminding Ken of a picture he'd seen once of a cormorant. Then the possibility that someone else in the family might take a fancy to his meal galvanized the bird to greater effort, and the whole fish vanished.

Ken and Giles watched the kingfishers until cramp and stiffness forced both of them to leave the blind for a good stretch and a scratch.

"They'll be gone soon, those young ones," Giles said. "They can fly a little bit already. They'll soon be away."

"What will they do then?"

"Establish their own territory. Find their own mates. Dig out nests for next year's broods."

"I hope we come here next year," Ken said.

"The kingfishers will be here if you do," Giles assured him. "It's their island. If there's a bad winter some are bound to die off, but there are always kingfishers on the island."

"Shall we go swimming now?" Ken suggested, and Giles laughed.

"You hoping for the Olympics?" he teased. "Come on then."

They got into the water on the sunny side of the island, and Ken practiced hard, became more and more adept, really enjoying himself. He was now brave enough to go out of his depth.

"What would you do if I started to sink?" he puffed to Giles, who was swimming easily alongside.

"This," said Giles, and diving like a duck, came up below Ken, deftly turned him onto his back, seized him under the armpits, and towed him to the bank.

"That was great," said Ken. "How do you swim on your back like that?"

Giles showed him, and Ken found that even pleasanter than the breaststroke he'd been practicing.

They swam together to Swan Island then, and Giles showed Ken the swans' nests, but they kept very circumspectly away from a big cob swan who was guarding his mate as she dozed with her head under her wing.

"Is it true they could break your leg?" Ken asked.

"I don't know," Giles said. "But if they come after your boat when they're angry, with those great wings beating the water, you don't take chances.

The best thing is to lie flat and wait till they've gone away. I always feel this old fellow knows me, but he knows I respect him too. She's his second wife, you know."

"Oh?" That sounded too much like a human situation to be true of a bird.

"They mate for life, swans do, but his mate swallowed a fishhook some idiot left in the reeds. My father took it out, but the wound went poisonous and she died. The old cob swam up and down, up and down, looking for her. You've never seen a creature so miserable. He was solitary a long while, but he's taken up with this young pen now, and seems content."

The female swan stirred in her sleep, flexed a wing and furled it again. The cob arched his sinuous neck over her, protectively, and then spoiled the effect of regal dignity by scratching the side of his head with his black, webbed foot.

"Let's go back to the punt now," Giles suggested, "and then go farther upstream to eat, and then drift down on the current later, when we're feeling lazy."

"O.K.," said Ken.

He had never been so far beyond Eight Island before, and it was all new country to him. The banks grew even more thickly with reeds and wild flowers, and there were stumpy, cut-back willows, the ugly sisters of the elegant, trailing trees farther downstream. These were all gnarled and knobbly, like great arthritic hands, and leafy shoots stood stiff as surprised hair. It was much more open here, and that much the hotter, and the river seemed more a creature of itself, a live thing, not just a place for play, and idling, and swimming. Somewhere, miles and miles away, it too had its secret springs, its dark beginnings, like the stream they had explored.

"Here's a good place," Giles suggested. A field had been cut for hay to the edge: a narrow field with a little wood beyond it. The bank curved inward slightly, as if it had once been a drinking place, but it was all grassed over now, making a series of turfy platforms between the top of the bank and the water's edge.

When they had tied up the punt, Ken sat on one of these platforms and dangled his feet. The water was very shallow, and his toes stirred the mud, staining the clear water with whorls of brown, like the pattern in a glass marble.

"Let's make a fire," Giles suggested.

"We've nothing to cook," said Ken.

"Doesn't matter. Just for fun."

"All right then."

They ran across the field and climbed the fence

into the wood, where there were plenty of sticks under the trees, and some larch cones, and a piece of an old dead silver birch tree, from which Giles stripped the papery bark in long curls.

They built a small fire by the water's edge, and Ken found some matches among the amazing paraphernalia that always seemed to accumulate in his various pockets. The smell of the burning bark as it flared to kindle the twigs around it was the essence of that day whenever he recalled it. The small flames were brilliant and clear, and the smoke hardly more than a heat shimmer, their fuel was so dry. Giles made a pile of twigs and cones at the top of the bank, and then the two boys squatted like a pair of Indian chiefs, and ate their meal.

Later, Giles seemed restless, and said he was going to walk along the bank, but Ken felt too lazy to stir.

"It's hot," he said. "I'm going to lie in the water."

"Well, don't try swimming without me," Giles said. "You'll get the cramp with all that chicken and cake in your stomach. You're greedy, old Mole."

Ken chucked a handful of pebbles at Giles, but he dodged and ran.

"Skinnyribs," Ken yelled after him.

When Giles was out of sight, Ken eased himself

down into the water and sprawled in the shallows. He had stripped and lay naked as an eel, his hands clasped behind his neck. He looked at the whole length of his body shimmering under the surface. The water was like a cool skin, wrapping and containing him. All around him the afternoon murmured and drowsed, and the air on his face was amazingly hot, while he lay in his cool cocoon of water. He opened and closed his toes and fingers, to let the coolness between them.

There would never be a moment in his life, he realized, when he would feel exactly as happy, exactly in the same way, as now. Even as you felt it, each particular happiness was evaporating, and could only be replaced by a different kind, or by something else altogether. It came to him that nothing can last for more than the fleeting second you are aware of it, and tomorrow's awareness is never the same as today's. Tomorrow, you were never quite the same person. No, nothing lasts: not life, not friendship, not the summer, not the moment, but moves on to what comes next. He was surprised that he found this a comforting rather than a melancholy thought.

Suddenly, something hit him on the nose. Giles, from the bank above, was throwing larch cones at him.

"Lazy dog! You've let the fire go nearly out. You were so quiet down there I thought you'd fallen asleep. What were you thinking about?"

"Dunno, really," said Ken. "Wondering why people get bored when there's so much to do."

"You weren't doing much of it," said Giles.

"Oh, you know what I mean."

Giles looked at him teasingly and recited in a prissy voice,

*"The world is so full of a number of things
I'm sure we should all be as happy as kings."*

Ken leaped up out of the water, grabbed Giles by the ankle and pulled him down the bank, where they wallowed and splashed in the water so much they entirely extinguished the fire.

"That's that, then," said Giles. "Come on then, Mole, let's float down as far as the day takes us."

They drifted down with the current as Ken had seen Giles do just a few days previously. It was as pleasurable as he had thought then that it must be.

"Why have you got that idiotic look on your face?" Giles asked. Ken began to chuckle quietly to himself.

"I'm the Lady of Shallott," he said.

" 'God in His mercy lend her grace,' " said Giles. "You look more like a turnip-head to me, or a beetroot. A boiled beetroot."

The punt lurched and wallowed as its two occupants developed their vegetable argument, but it was too hot to continue for long, and anyway they needed to look to their paddles as a racing four came speeding upstream, all muscle and sweat and grunting breath, and expecting such lowly craft as punts to dispatch themselves out of the way.

They collected the canoe from Eight Island and traveled alongside each other. Ken felt he was ready to try the canoe and Giles promised to look over the one in the Lawnside boathouse.

"If it's O.K. it'll be more fun to take them both out; if not, we'll double up in mine."

When they had moored the punt, Ken went up to the house, calling Giles after him.

"Mrs. Morris can't believe you really got me swimming," he said. "She thinks you're a miracle."

"So I am," said Giles, modestly.

The house was empty, though, rather to Ken's surprise. It looked exactly as it had when he left that morning, as if no one had been near, yet it was after five o'clock: nearer six in fact. They'd been longer upriver than Ken had realized. He was puzzling about where Mrs. Morris might be when the phone rang.

"Is that you, dear?" a voice asked him.

"Yes, it's me, Mrs. Morris. Where are you?"

"Still with my niece. The baby hasn't arrived yet, so I'll have to stay with her. I really am sorry, Ken. I don't know what your parents will think, me leaving you on your own like this, but she's scared silly, poor girl. I tell her, we all came the same way, so she's not the first one to put up with having a baby, but she's asked to have me with her."

"I'll be all right, Mrs. Morris. Really. Don't worry about me. And Mother and Father won't know."

"Thanks, dear. Take care now."

"All right. Good-bye, Mrs. Morris," said Ken. "I hope she has a nice baby."

"She won't be back for ages," Ken told Giles. "Her niece is having a baby."

"Come on then," said Giles. "We'll look at that canoe."

After a very thorough inspection Giles declared that it was sound enough.

"She's a wee bit heavier than mine, but you'll manage her O.K. once you get the feel of it. She'll be very different from the punt, mind."

Ken felt very unsafe at first. Knowing that he could swim now, though still not very strongly, was a great help, but he still wasn't sure how he'd react if he went suddenly and involuntarily under. The canoe seemed very unstable, shifting alarmingly to every movement he made, reacting almost too quickly to each thrust of the paddle.

Giles, walking along the stone edge to reach his own canoe, called out to him to put the life jacket on.

"Where is it?"

"I chucked it in behind you."

Putting it on was about as easy as doing a strip-tease on a tightrope, but it was reassuring to be wearing it.

"Where shall we go?" called Giles.

"Down to the lock?"

"All right then."

Giles paddled alongside like a mother duck watching her brood. Ken, once he got the hang of the canoe, found it a deal more fun than the punt.

"What shall we do tomorrow, Giles?" he called. Giles was looking in his direction, but seemed abstracted.

"What?" he said.

"I was just wondering about tomorrow."

"I'm not sure. I don't know how much longer I shall be staying."

"Oh. I see."

Ken paddled along in silence. He did not want

Giles to go. He wanted to say, "Do you *have* to go?" but couldn't bring himself to. He wanted to ask him *where* he was going and what he'd be doing and whether he'd be back, but somehow Giles didn't invite questioning. He told you what he wanted to tell you, and no more.

It was impossible to be dispirited for long, though, as they cruised on in the direction of the lock, but something caught their attention before they got there. Tied up to the prohibitory bank of the empty Georgian house was the scruffy cabin cruiser *Adventurer*, and there was no one aboard her.

"What do you think?" Giles asked.

Ken looked at the boat and then at the house, and saw movement inside one of the unshuttered windows.

"Stoats and weasels," he said.

Giles grinned at him and raised an agreeing thumb. They tucked their canoes quietly alongside the bank and moored them. Giles got out first and helped Ken up, and they crept quietly toward the house under cover of the shrubbery. There were cigarette packets and chocolate papers littered about, and the summerhouse door had been wrenched open. Several deck chairs and a sun bed had been set up and obviously sat in.

Now they were closer, Ken could hear the sound of voices and music coming from inside the house. Ken felt that it probably served the owners right, leaving the place and going off somewhere else. He felt an irrational dislike for these rich people he'd never met who cluttered up their expensive river frontage with notices telling you what not to do. The people from the *Adventurer* had probably made a bit of a mess, but what would that matter? Money would put that right in no time.

The glass in the French windows had been smashed, so as to undo the bolts, and the gaping space made the sound of voices and the thump and twang of a guitar all the louder. Ken peered cautiously in.

"God!" he said. It was appalling. Every piece of furniture had been upended and smashed, and a pretty little inlaid chess table, the nearest thing to where Ken stood, was scarred with burn marks.

Someone had sprayed obscenities all over the walls in red and purple paint. There were beer cans everywhere. The canvas of a picture had stab marks all over it. Three girls were sitting smoking on a pile of sofa cushions; a man was accompanying the guitar player by beating out a rhythm on the parquet flooring with a hammer. Another man was peeing in the corner. There was an awful smell of filth and a sweetish stink from the cigarette smoke. Ken suspected someone had been sick somewhere.

"We'd better go. Quick!" whispered Giles, but one of the girls caught sight of Ken and shrieked. He turned and ran, aware of movement in the house, knowing they would be after him.

"Giles! Where are you?" He was confused and afraid, and took the nearest path, blindly, running and running, with a clatter of heavy footsteps behind him. He was on the path to the boathouse: no way out. The high prim hedges penned him in. Then he saw that the inner gates of the boathouse had been wrenched open. Someone had taken an axe to the little launch, and the rowing boat was sunk to its gunwales.

Ken leaped in, expecting shallow water like the Lawnside boathouse, but it came up to his armpits and the mud was thick, clinging to his ankles and sending up oily bubbles. He swam two strokes to the outer gates, but these were still securely locked. Beyond, on the river, Giles had brought the canoes around and, sitting in one, held the other by its line like a led horse.

"This way, Ken!" he called out.

"I can't. I can't, it's locked. They're coming." He was in a shivering sweat of panic and his mind would not clear and show him what to do.

"Dive under the gates, Ken! Now! Come on!"

Giles's voice carried clear across the water, piercing Ken's confusion. Driven by fear greater than his fear of submerging himself in that black water, he gulped in air, and duck-dived, as he had seen Giles do so often. Up he bobbed on the other side like a cork, gratefully breathed again, and felt Giles heave him into the other canoe. In the distance, coming nearer, they could hear the sound of police cars.

"I want to be sick," said Ken.

"You'll be all right," Giles told him. "Sit still a moment, and breathe slow and easy. Then we'd better go home."

Ken half hoped Giles might offer to stay overnight with him, but he continued upstream when they had got the Lawnside canoe safely in her boathouse. He turned and waved when he was some distance away, and Ken moved back and stood and watched him go. His eyes retained the image of Giles's outline against the low sun minutes after the canoe had rounded the curve of the river to be hidden by the reeds on the far bank.

"Good night," Ken called out across the water, and, "Good night," a voice called back again. The sound echoed off the river and vanished. Everything was silent. It took Ken a while to shake himself out of his thoughts. Then, because the evening was so warm, he decided to fetch his bedding from the house and sleep in the tent, to let the fresh air blow away the memory of that stinking ravaged house down the river.

Stars began to show in the sky, though there were clouds building up on the horizon. Perhaps the weather was due to break.

He got into his sleeping bag, not for warmth, as the night was so hot, but because it made a small friendly place in the largeness of the night. Words came into his head about the stars:

> *I will not believe that starshine*
> *Is only spent light from dead spheres.*
> *Even if it is true I will not believe it.*
> *They are not burnt out, but burning*
> *Still in their far places.*

He was very tired, and fell asleep with his mind on stars.

Seven

He woke in one of the hours to either side of midnight. It was the still not-quite-dark of a summer night, and everything had a very queer look about it. It was as if the whole landscape were an image reflected in polished steel: darkly bright, if such a thing is possible. The air was hot, heavy, and electric. It made Ken's skin prickle. A high bank of black cloud brooded over the trees beyond the river.

Everything waited. Then, at last, the first fizzing whiteness of lightning and the artillery-burst of thunder that followed surprised and relieved him at the same time, breaking the tension. He huddled the sleeping bag around him, and from the frail safety of his tent settled back to watch the storm, elated by it even while it scared him, as if he was watching a terrifying film. The lightning appeared to be doubled by the water as it leaped down to its own reflection. The willow branches flickered a garish yellow-green in the momentary light. With each flash, the garden became a stage set, harshly lit and unreal, making the intervening darkness deeper and more opaque.

Suddenly, rain came hissing toward Ken from the opposite bank of the river, splattering down into the water, pocking the smooth surface, advancing on him until it was hammering at the tent roof. The noise was terrific, but he exulted in it, and shouted against the storm. It was the most marvelous thing in the world to be in this small, safe space in the middle of it all. The big guns boomed and spat like a sea battle, and the rain kept up its bombardment. Even bigger drops were bounding back from the river now, making sizeable depressions that rippled and ringed outward in all directions, mazing the water with conflicting patterns.

For almost half an hour the storm lasted, and Ken lay there, hardly moving, except to arch his arms over his head when a particularly violent thunderclap burst over him. It would not have occurred to him to run for shelter indoors. It did not matter that he was afraid. It was magnificent.

He wondered what Giles was doing; imagined the kingfishers, huddled in their nesting hole, and the swans on their platform of sedges. Were they used to the storm, accepting it, or did the cob spread his great wings and challenge it, as he would challenge any other danger to his mate?

All along the river, creatures must be huddled against the storm. Those underground would be the luckiest. What if you were a fox or a badger out hunting on a night like this though, seeing your dim, accustomed, nocturnal world lit up so suddenly by these intermittent flashes? Were foxes afraid of thunder as dogs were? Mother's old dog used to howl all the time during a storm. Ken recalled the chilling noise of it.

Gradually the thunder died away, leaving only the steady rhythm of the falling rain to disturb the now cooler night. It continued its drumming on the canvas, but the tent was proof against it. Not a drop of water got in. If it hadn't leaked by now it certainly would keep him dry till morning.

Ken began to drift and dream. The storm became a memory. The warmth from the sleeping bag was just right. The garden breathed out the beautiful smell of rain. It had been dry too long, and the roots would be thankful for the wet.

Ken woke again in the first early light to find the rain stopped and the sky clear, and thought about how he would spend the day. If Giles was really going soon he'd better get up to Eight Island before long and ask him when. There had been no sign of packing yesterday, no suggestion of things got ready for leaving, but he had *said* he'd be going. Too early to disturb him yet, though.

The air was cool. Water drops hung on every twig and leaf and web and petal that Ken could see. He did not want to lie in the tent any longer. He was restless and would rather be up and doing. He wanted to take the canoe out, to practice the new skill he had learned, so he dressed quickly and went down to the boathouse, and pushed out onto the river. It was very, very quiet, as though the day had scarcely begun to breathe; had just begun to exhale fine swirls of mist from the river's surface. He hardly liked to disturb it by the dipping of his paddle, and let the canoe drift, moving himself only enough to keep her course straight.

The ducks eyed him sleepily from the bank, and an owl, late home from hunting, delayed perhaps by the storm, planed across the water to a tree stump and glared suspiciously at this early riser. It ruffled its feathers and moved its head as if its neck were a universal joint. It was a good trick. Ken wished he could do it.

All the houses were shut and sleeping. All the gardens were deserted. Storm-soaked flowers drooped heavily in the borders. The place of the boys' frightening adventure had been washed clean by the storm, Ken felt, as he passed by. Not really, of course. The filth and destruction would still be there. Who would clean it up, he wondered. Somebody, surely, before the owners came back. Certainly the wind had blown away the litter from the lawn. Ken shivered, and urged the canoe on past. Someone else was up on the river, he discovered. The young woman on the houseboat was washing down the little motorboat *Cygnet* that was tied up alongside.

"Morning," she called.

"Hello!" said Ken. He thought she'd probably say "You're up early" or something obvious like that, but she didn't.

He could see from where he was that the lock was closed and the curtains firmly drawn in the keeper's cottage. There was no one around yet to disturb him. Ken saw the "DANGER" sign where the water drew on to where the weir began. It was nailed to the first of a row of stout, white-painted posts, with a broad beam running along the top of them, like a gigantic, one-railed fence. If you could balance well, you could walk the beam from the signpost to the lock edge, and boats could moor along its length when the lock was very busy.

Carefully Ken maneuvered the canoe across, though he was a little nervous when he saw how the river's speed increased at this point, and felt the pull of it against the paddle. He was determined to get a look at the weir, though. The noise of it was louder now, as it took the storm water away past the lock. He tied the canoe firmly to a post, and climbed gingerly onto the beam, sitting astride it, not trusting his balance, for the flowing water made him giddy if he looked down at it too long.

Now he could see the edge of the weir, where the water poured over, gray-green at the lip and then vanishing into white foam. There was something very exciting about the racing water, but it made Ken nervous, all the same. He was glad he had seen it, but he had seen enough. He climbed back into the canoe, and was just going to loose her when he heard the sound of an engine: erratic, misfiring, and then fading altogether. It was the *Cygnet* coming toward him, and her owner was trying to get the engine to fire again. The bows were beginning to swing over, to follow the current, to head for the weir.

He thought he might paddle out to her, and try to pull her back, but it would be more likely the *Cygnet* would just tow the canoe after her. The girl was concentrating on the engine: hadn't yet seen Ken. He climbed onto the beam again and hoped she'd come close enough for his second idea to work. He waved and called, "Oy! *Cygnet*. Throw me a line, quick!"

The girl looked up, saw him, and picked up a long coil of light rope from the decking. Ken hoped he would catch it and not make a fool of himself. She flung the line and he reached for it. The relief of the sting of it against his hand was incredible, and he snubbed it quickly about the "DANGER" post and secured it. The *Cygnet* ran on until the line stopped her like a dog on the end of its lead, and the girl hauled her in, hand over hand, until she could be tied up to the beam, opposite Ken's canoe.

"Thank you," the girl said. "She'd have smashed up if I'd gone over there."

"What's wrong with the engine?" Ken asked.

"Too much choke, I think. I should know better. I was in a bit of a rush. I'd promised Bill I'd wake him this morning. His alarm's gone wrong."

"Bill?"

"The lockkeeper. Will you wait here a moment? I'll go and shout to him."

She gave Ken no time to answer but ran off down the beam as easily as if it were a pavement. Ken waited: He heard her call out, and saw the cottage bedroom window open in response. When she came back she said, "I don't know your name, do I? I'm Jill Brett."

"I'm Ken Holmes," he said. They shook hands.

"I'll try the engine again now," she said. "But I'll leave her tied till I'm sure she'll behave herself. I'm not courting disaster again, even with my gallant rescuer so close at hand."

She was grinning at him, but she was not teasing. Girls in general were teasing, cliquish sort of cattle, he usually found. They either ignored you, or tried to claim you as if you were some sort of trophy. They made Ken uneasy, but Jill Brett didn't. Her gratitude was genuine, even if she did joke about it. Not that he wanted gratitude, mind.

"I expect you'd have been all right, anyway," he said. She became serious then.

"Don't you believe it," she said. "It's a bad weir, this one, when the river's high. One or two boats have gone over. About three years ago four people were drowned here."

"That's awful," Ken said.

"It was. There was a man with a couple of kids in a rowboat. He could handle the boat all right, but they think he must have had some kind of seizure. A brilliant man, apparently, quite a well-known naturalist. Some people saw the boat overturn and went to the rescue, and then a boy turned up in a canoe. It was his father in the boat, and his brothers. He could swim like a fish, it seems, this lad, and he dived and dived to find them, and brought one little boy out, dead, and someone else found the other child, drowned too, and their brother went down again to look for his father. The boy must have been exhausted. He was dead as well when they pulled them both out of the water."

Ken sat and stared at his feet. He could not say anything. Jill Brett looked at his white face and saw that she had shocked him with her telling of the tragedy. He looked as shattered as if he were in some way personally involved. It had taken a good deal of nerve to balance himself on the beam and grab a rope from the *Cygnet* and hang on as he had. He was more shaken than she'd realized, and she was sorry about it.

"Come back to the houseboat," she said. "Unless someone's expecting you. We'll have breakfast."

The engine was running healthily now, so they tied the canoe to the stern of the *Cygnet* and headed for the boathouse, with Jill Brett talking about any topic under the sun as long as it wasn't weirs, and drownings.

She gave him a good breakfast: hot chocolate, and rolls and butter, and dark chunky marmalade that said it had rum in it.

"I saw you the other day, didn't I?" she asked, as they sat under the awning where he had first seen her.

"We'd been down by the lock," he said.

"We?"

"A friend of mine. A boy I met."

"Call in here, any time you're passing," she said. "I'm here all summer. I fish a bit sometimes. I don't catch much. You could join me if you'd nothing better to do."

It was a pleasant, easy invitation. He knew she meant it, but she wasn't pressing him. He thought he'd probably come again. Later on, maybe.

"I'd better go now," he said. "They'll be missing me." She untied the canoe for him, and waved as he paddled off upriver.

Lawnside still looked deserted. He paddled on to Eight Island. It would be a much cooler day.

There were rags of clouds about in the sky. The swans were watchful as he passed their nesting place, and he caught no glimpse of the kingfishers.

The house on Eight Island seemed more swallowed up in its leafy, weedy garden than ever, and he knew beyond any least shadow of doubt that Giles was not there. No point in getting out onto the creaking boards of the landing stage, or walking along the mossy, brambly path to the door. The whole place proclaimed to him that it was no longer occupied. A hollow sadness, a sense of desolation, crept into the corners of Ken's mind. He would not see Giles again. Then the canoe moved under him, as if to remind him of his new skills, to shame him from his despondency. He tucked his paddle under the stern and swung the boat around. He did not look back at Eight Island, but paddled on downstream, and with the exercise of his new skill gradually became content again, and more than content, and he smiled to himself, and thought that later on he'd go for a swim.

Having worked away his melancholy, he began to paddle more slowly, looking about him at all the now-familiar features of the riverside. He noticed that even now, perhaps because of the long hot days, some of the trees were tinged with yellow, as if they were already tired of summer. He had weeks yet to spend, but it would not be the same river. If he were to return next year, it would be different again. Sometimes things would remind him of what it had been like though, and he was glad of that.

Then, once again he quickened the pace of his paddle, and watched the little bow wave go dancing out from either side of him. He began to sing to himself, in time with the rhythm of the blade. So occupied was he with his singing that he almost missed what he had waited so long to see. For a second or so, out of the corner of his eye, he registered the presence of a brown sleek shape in the water, with a broad flat head, dark eyes, and whiskered nose. The otter surfaced briefly and regarded Ken, and Ken looked back at the otter. Then it vanished. He wished Giles had seen it.

As Ken brought the canoe toward Lawnside he saw someone standing in the garden, and something grew uncomfortable in him as he realized it was his father. They must have got back earlier than they'd thought. He wondered if Mrs. Morris was back; where Mother was; whether there'd been a row about his not being there. His heart began to thump in anticipation of a telling-off, of his first contact with his parents being a cause for upset and blame.

Just for a moment he became the person he had been a week or so ago. Then a grin spread across his face as he saw his father turn and catch sight of the approaching canoe. From the veranda Ken's mother was stepping down into the garden, and Mrs. Morris was with her, engrossed in conversation. Probably telling her all about the baby. He supposed Mrs. M.'s niece must have *had* the baby by now. He really wasn't sure how long these things took.

The two women weren't looking in his direction. They were walking toward the tent as if expecting to find him there. All three of them gave the impression of having only just arrived, and the two women of not yet having discovered his absence, and he was about to be present again, so it hardly mattered now.

He purposely did not hurry, but brought the canoe along in a good straight course, manipulating the paddle as Giles had taught him. It gave him time for appraisal of his father standing there on the bank, looking gray and familiar and most rewardingly amazed. Even if the amazement were to turn to irritability, like a coach to a pumpkin, it wouldn't matter. Ken had seen it. He brought the canoe skillfully alongside the stone edge of the Lawnside garden, took hold of the mooring ring, and shipped his paddle.

"Hello, Father," he said.